MAFIA CAPTIVE

Mafia Ménage Trilogy #1

JULIA SYKES

Copyright © 2021 by Julia Sykes

All rights reserved.

No part of this book may be reproduced in any form or by any electronic or mechanical means, including information storage and retrieval systems, without written permission from the author, except for the use of brief quotations in a book review.

Cover image: Wander Aguiar Photography

Cover design: Popkitty Design

Chapter One
JOSEPH

I knew I was dangerously close to crossing a line. I shouldn't touch her: the barely legal, innocent angel who'd captivated my attention from the first moment her lovely blue eyes had met mine.

Ashlyn. She had no ties to my dark world. It was selfish and reckless for me to allow myself to get close to her.

But when she swayed toward me, as though drawn by the same magnetic pull that'd been tempting and tormenting me for weeks, she was nearly impossible to resist.

I should've walked away. I should've ignored her, rejected her. Bruising her pride now might save her from bruises marring her alabaster skin in the future.

My fists curled as the gruesome, stomach-churning image of her in pain flashed across my mind. Any association with me could put her at risk. If someone from my former life tracked me down, she'd be targeted to draw me out. To punish me.

I'd ached to claim the gorgeous, curvy brunette ever since she'd peeked up at me from across the dingy bar where I worked. The place was a dive, but college students didn't come here for pretentious cocktails; the owner didn't care if his customers were underage, and he didn't mind paying me cash under the table. I'd chosen this job because it allowed me anonymity. There was no official record of my employment, no digital trail to betray my location. No one could find me here. Not my brutal allies or my sadistic enemies.

If I were a good man, I'd spare Ashlyn from the taint of my gritty world; a world someone like her—with her pretty, charmed life—would never understand.

I'd resolved to put that world in my past, but that didn't mean it couldn't catch up to me at any time. I was on the run, most likely being hunted by my so-called *family*.

They were the least of my worries. If my family's enemies caught up to me, anyone close to me would be in danger.

I didn't want that for Ashlyn. But every time she

stepped into the bar, my hunger for her grew sharper. She was stunning, but it wasn't simply her beauty that entranced me. During our brief encounters, her cheeks flushed the prettiest shade of pink, and her long lashes lowered to hide the desire that darkened her eyes.

She was soft, sweet, and shy—all the feminine qualities that called to the most perverse aspects of my nature.

Back home, I was used to getting what I wanted. My family had more money than we could ever possibly spend, and women were eager to fall into my bed. They were drawn to my wealth and my power.

That'd never bothered me before. I'd never really thought about it at all.

Until Ashlyn looked at me with raw desire. *Me.* Not an obscenely rich heir who might shower her with expensive gifts. Ashlyn didn't have any ulterior motive for wanting me. This was simple, animal attraction. It was a tempting glimpse at the life I craved: one that was entirely ordinary, untouched by violence and vicious power plays.

A life where I didn't have innocent blood on my hands.

But even as I entertained the impossible fantasy of dating her like I was a normal man with an unremarkable past, I knew there was nothing ordinary about the intensity of our connection. This kind of burning, consuming chemistry was rare. Stronger than anything I'd ever felt before.

Over the long weeks of self-denial, she'd become so much more than a beautiful woman I desperately wanted to claim. I'd placed her on a pedestal in my mind: the perfect, sweet angel with the perfect, sweet life. I envied her and craved her at the same time. If I could touch her, taste her, I might be able to pretend that kind of life could be mine, just for a moment.

I knew I was poison to her, but I wasn't sure how much longer I could restrain my darkest, hungriest impulses.

Chapter Two
ASHLYN

My stomach did a funny little flip when his eyes met mine. Although the bar was crowded with intoxicated students, the cacophony of feminine laughter and hip-hop music faded away. The phenomenon was familiar, and I found it addictive. I found these moments with *him* addictive. His cocky, crooked smile made my heart race and my blood heat.

I leaned on the bar that separated me from Joseph, my body swaying toward his without conscious thought. We'd only ever exchanged the briefest physical contact when he pressed free drinks into my hand, his long fingers brushing against mine.

I was crushing hard on the breathtaking bartender, but so were most of the women who frequented the dive bar where it was easy to get served underage. While I wasn't usually one to bat my lashes and flirt my way into free drinks, the connection I felt to Joseph was electric. I wasn't intentionally acting coy; I simply couldn't resist the chemistry between us.

And although he always lingered when he served me drinks with that heart-stopping smile and those dancing aquamarine eyes, I couldn't tell if the attraction was one-sided. He likely flirted with most of the girls in the bar. After all, he was trying to get tips.

"Same as usual, Ashlyn?" His velvety voice caressed my name, thrumming deeper than the heavy bassline that pulsed through the bar.

"Um, yes, please," I breathed. I was far from composed, but I couldn't help getting hot and flustered when he captured me in his intense, flame-blue gaze. With his dark eyelashes and sensual mouth, his features might have seemed almost feminine. But the sharp line of his stubble-covered jaw and defined cheekbones were decidedly masculine. His black hair curled slightly around his chiseled face. I craved to run my fingers through it, to see if it was as thick and soft as it appeared.

His eyes finally dropped from mine as he filled a small plastic cup with ice, poured a generous measure of orange vodka, and topped it with cranberry juice. I sucked in a breath when he released me from his gaze, and my own hungry stare drifted lower as I admired the way his muscles bulged and flexed beneath his indecently tight black t-shirt.

My tongue darted out to wet my lips. I could feel his eyes burning into me once again, and I realized he'd noticed my wanton reaction to him. My cheeks flamed, and I stared at the highly polished bar top.

He set the drink in front of me, but he didn't draw away. His hand lingered on the cup, waiting for me to take it. I peeked up at him, wondering for the hundredth time if there was more to his flirtatious behavior than a desire for a tip.

My fingers trembled slightly as I reached for the drink, anticipating the physical contact. When my hand closed around the chilled cup, he slid his fingers between mine. The light glide of his calloused skin made my flesh pebble, and I suppressed a shiver.

"Hey, are you done?" An annoyed, feminine voice sounded from behind me.

I jolted away from Joseph, the moment shattered. My embarrassment surged in a searing wave, and I tossed a five-dollar bill into the tip jar before darting away, nearly spilling my beverage as I hastened to put distance between us.

I weaved through the crowd, returning to Jayme. My best friend leaned on a high table in the back corner, smirking at me. My body still burned with mortification and something darker that I chose to ignore. I could barely meet her sparkling green eyes.

She flipped her long blonde hair over her shoulder and addressed me drily. "So, where's my drink?"

Crap.

I'd been so flustered by my body's helpless reaction to Joseph that I'd forgotten to get a vodka-cranberry for my friend, too.

"Sorry," I muttered. "I, um, got distracted."

"Of course you did. Hottie McHotstuff was practically eye-fucking you for five minutes. When are you going to hit that, girl?"

I shook my head. Jayme might be completely confident when it came to ensnaring men—different guys rotated in and out of our apartment on a regular basis—but I was more reserved. Well, to be honest, I was shy. And wary, after being cheated on by my boyfriend last year. I was what Jayme termed a *serial monogamist.* I didn't trust easily, so when I finally did start to open up to someone, I committed fully.

Jimmy cheating on me had set me back even further when it came to trust issues.

"You're crazy for not tapping that," Jayme declared. "You know Joseph would come home with you if you invited him. Let's stay until close, and then you can make your move."

I rolled my eyes. "You know that won't happen. I wish you wouldn't tease me about it."

She held up her hands in a show of contrition. "I'm not teasing. I'm trying to get you some well-deserved action."

I blew out a sigh. I couldn't put myself on the line like that, especially when I feared rejection. Jayme seemed sure that my invitation would be accepted, but I wasn't so certain. I still wasn't convinced that Joseph was truly interested in me.

She made a little waving motion, shifting the subject. "Okay, let's start with an easier mark, then. You *know* Stu is into you. You kissed at that house party last weekend. He's kind of an entitled douche, but he's hot. It's not like you have to marry him or anything." She smirked on the last, teasing just a little.

My pulse stuttered, but not in the same way Joseph affected me. This was a nervous reaction. The last time I'd been with Stu, he'd provided me with a steady supply of some mystery cocktail that'd been strong enough to burn my throat with every sip. I'd known it was highly alcoholic, but I'd overindulged to counteract my social anxiety. By the end of the night, I'd been rolling my hips while dancing with wild abandon, and Stu had moved in. I'd kissed him in a drunken frenzy in the middle of the party.

It wasn't like me to behave that way, and I was deeply embarrassed by the memory. Jayme was right. I'd been a while since I'd gotten intimate with a guy, and the alcohol in my system had loosened my inhibitions too much.

"I'm not proud of that," I said truthfully.

"So, you don't like him?"

I shrugged. Stu was conventionally attractive, but he didn't make my heart race and my belly clench.

Jayme gave me a sly smile. "Well, you'd better make up your mind fast, because he's on his way over here." She pushed away from the table. "I'm going to get a drink. I'll be back soon. Maybe. Probably not. Get it, girl."

"Jayme," I said sharply. She simply grinned and slipped into the crowd.

"Hey, Ashlyn. You need a drink?" I recognized Stu's voice behind me.

I closed my eyes for a moment and took a breath before turning to face him. I managed a polite smile and raised my full cup. "I'm good," I assured him. "But thanks."

"Next one's on me." He flashed a wide, boyish grin. With his dark blond hair and forest green eyes, Stu was cute in a clean-cut, preppy way. He wore a slightly formal blue button-up shirt and boat shoes, exuding casual country-club vibes.

Preppy and entitled wasn't my usual type, but he was undeniably charming.

"I'm glad I caught you here tonight. I've been wanting to ask you something," he said, still grinning that cocky grin.

"Yeah?" I shifted on my feet, and my fingers twined together in an unconscious nervous tic. If he was about to ask me back to his place, I was going to have to deal with the awkwardness of turning him down. No matter how long it'd been since I'd slept with a guy, I wasn't interested in casual sex.

"We're hosting a party at the Fly clubhouse next weekend. I want you to be my date." His chin tipped back slightly, his posture swelling with pride and a touch of haughtiness.

The Fly was one of the prestigious, exclusive final clubs at Harvard. It was kind of a big deal that Stu was a member. And it was kind of a big deal for him to invite me, especially since I didn't really run in those circles. My introverted nature had made the vetting process for final clubs far too daunting to consider, and I'd assumed they weren't going to be part of my Harvard experience.

It would be cool to see the inside of the clubhouse, but Stu wasn't exactly asking me to be his date. More like he was making an announcement.

Even though these parties could be infamously decadent, I wasn't very impressed with his attitude.

"Oh," I managed, stalling. Stu's demeanor rubbed me the wrong way, but I really was tempted to go to the party.

His brows rose, and one corner of his mouth ticked up in a teasing smile. "Oh? Is that a *yes*?"

Definitely cocky. But there was a touch of uncertainty in his eyes that softened my irritation. He didn't want to be rejected by me any more than I wanted to be rejected by Joseph. At least Stu had the guts to ask me out, unlike me when it came to making a move on Joseph.

I smiled up at him. "Sure. I'll be your date."

Even though I wasn't interested in him romantically, dressing up and getting an inside look at the Fly clubhouse would be fun. And like Jayme said, I didn't have to marry him. It was just a date, not a promise for a long-term relationship.

"But only if Jayme can come too," I added with forced assertiveness. Not only did I need my bestie as an anxiety buffer, but she would be even more thrilled to attend the party than I was.

Stu returned my smile with a triumphant grin, and his gaze left mine to search for Jayme. When he caught sight of her, his eyes flicked up and down her body, appraising. "For sure. There's always room on the guest list for beautiful ladies."

I smothered a frown. I didn't love the idea that Jayme and I might've been invited to the event only because the guys wanted to pack the room with women for them to ogle.

Stu's grin turned sharp enough to make me edge away on instinct. I fought down the budding suspicion that female guests weren't invited solely to serve as arm candy. We were fresh meat.

This is just how it is, I reminded myself. Most students were desperate to attend these parties. The members could be as selective with the guest list as they wanted. Really, I should be flattered that Stu wanted me to come as his date. And it would be comforting to have Jayme with me. It was nice of Stu to include her so easily. Wasn't it?

He raised his beer and touched it to my cup, sealing our promised date with a celebratory "cheers." I realized I hadn't said anything for several seconds, so I hastily tipped my own drink back in response. He drained half his beer in a few long gulps, but I lowered mine after no more than a sip. I didn't want to get drunk and lose control again.

Stu's disconcerting energy was putting me on edge, and it would be far too easy to down my vodka in an attempt to soothe my mounting nervousness. I knew my anxiety level wasn't rational, and I wished Jayme was at my side. My bestie always grounded me when she sensed I was about to spiral.

My gaze flicked to the crowded dance floor, searching for her.

Stu snatched my attention back immediately, wrapping his hand around my chilled cup. His fingers closed over mine, but my small shudder at his touch was nothing like the shiver that Joseph had elicited. The gorgeous bartender's hand had been calloused and steady, his heat sinking into my skin to warm my insides. Stu's fingers were cold and clammy from holding his frosted pint glass.

Before I could recoil, he boldly firmed his grip and lifted my drink toward his lips. I gaped at him as he took a sip without asking. He didn't release my hand, holding my fingers captive around the cup.

Before I could formulate an indignant response, he grimaced and lowered the sweet drink. I huffed out a small, relieved breath when he finally slid his fingers from mine so that he could set my cup down on the high-topped table beside me.

"No wonder you're barely sipping that cheap shit." His nose wrinkled. "I know this place is a dive, but they could expand their liquor selection. My IPA is decent, though. We can share."

He lifted his glass and reached for me, trying to get me to mirror the way he'd tasted my drink.

I snatched my hand away before he could make contact. I didn't want to feel his clammy fingers clamp over mine again. "No, thanks."

"Come on, Ashlyn. Don't be like that."

I pressed my lips together and shook my head, not caring for the peer pressure.

He's just flirting, I told myself as I attempted to smother my unease. His proprietary touches were making my stomach knot, but that anxiety was unreasonable. Wasn't it?

Just last weekend, I'd practically wrapped myself around him while we made out. He wasn't some creepy stranger. There was no reason for me to interpret his nearness as anything other than confident flirtation.

I'd allowed him to get me drunk before, but I was more clearheaded this time. I didn't want to repeat the experience, and I definitely didn't want to repeat the wicked hangover.

"Okay, then." He set his beer down on the table. He was still smiling, and I managed a small smile in return.

I didn't want my anxiety to rule my life, and I knew I'd regret it if I allowed my nerves to ruin Stu's invite to the final club party. Jayme would be so excited when I gave her the news. I focused on my friend's happiness to dispel the weird vibes that were setting me on edge.

Suddenly, the stale scent of Stu's IPA washed over my face as he imposed himself in my personal space. I took an instinctive step back and bumped into the barstool behind me. I stumbled, and he caught my upper arms to prevent me from falling.

"Thanks," I mumbled, embarrassed. I tried to shift away again, but he didn't let me go.

"I think you owe me a kiss," he announced, leaning in so his hot breath fanned over my lips. He smelled like beer and cigarettes. My stomach twisted.

"I don't think so," I countered, trying to sound firmly assertive. Instead, the refusal came out a little breathlessly. Even though I'd kissed him before, I was distinctly uncomfortable with his nearness and his persistent grip on my arms.

"Don't be a cocktease. You know you want it."

My stomach churned as my anxiety soured into fear. This wasn't simply arrogant flirting. When we'd kissed in a drunken frenzy, his hands had been rough and groping, but I hadn't exactly been at my best, either. I'd dismissed his pawing as sloppy intoxication.

I wasn't sure if he was drunk right now, but there was no excuse for calling me a cocktease. My skin crawled where he maintained his firm grip on my upper arms.

"You're wrong," I insisted, barely managing to force more than a whispered denial up my constricted throat. "I don't want this. I want you to let me go." I tried to twist out of his hold, but he didn't release me. Instead, he leaned closer.

"Take your hands off her." The menace in the low, masculine growl made me shudder.

I looked past Stu with wide eyes, searching for my savior. Joseph's flame-blue gaze burned into the boy who'd trapped me. My mouth went dry, but his fury wasn't directed at me.

Stu finally let me go so he could face off against Joseph. I quickly put distance between us, my back hitting the wall after a few steps. Stu placed his body in front of mine, blocking me off in a clearly territorial demonstration.

"Get away from her." Joseph's voice was a low, fierce rumble. He had several inches of height on Stu, even though the preppy boy was a little over six feet tall. Joseph's impressive muscles rippled with barely restrained violence.

Stu was either drunk enough or stupid enough that he didn't back down.

"Fuck off," he sneered.

Joseph moved with lightning speed, and his fists

curled in the front of Stu's shirt. He jerked the boy away from me and slammed him back against the wall, forcing several feet of distance between us.

"Leave," he ordered coldly. "You're banned. If I ever see you in here again—and if I ever see you anywhere near Ashlyn—you'll answer to me."

He held Stu in his burning stare a few seconds longer, impressing his will on the smaller man. When he finally released him, Stu shoved at his rock-solid chest in a show of petulance. Joseph barely swayed back an inch, standing his ground. His eyes narrowed on Stu, and the creep shot one last glare in my direction before sulking off toward the exit.

"You okay?"

I jolted when Joseph addressed me. His low, soothing tone was in sharp contrast to the menace that had imbued his voice when he'd threatened Stu.

"Um, yeah." I realized I was trembling. I tried to still my shaking fingers. I wasn't hurt, but the encounter had been unnerving.

"I'm going to take you home." It wasn't a question, but I found myself nodding in response. I didn't want to leave without an escort in case Stu decided to wait for me outside.

The bar had gone quiet around us as all the focus shifted toward the altercation between Stu and Joseph. Dozens of eyes pricked at my skin like needles, and I was suddenly desperate to return to the safe solitude of my apartment.

"Come on. I've got you." Joseph reached out his hand, giving me the option to initiate physical contact. After Stu had inserted himself in my personal space, I appreciated that Joseph allowed me to choose whether or not I wanted him to touch me.

I wasn't at all afraid of him. How could I be, when he'd just swooped in and saved me like my own personal knight in shining armor? Although his assertion that he'd take me home had been firm, he was waiting for my consent.

I placed my hand in his, and a sense of safety rolled over me, easing the knots in my stomach. His long fingers closed around mine in a gentle grip. I breathed out a relieved sigh and gratefully followed him toward the exit. The crowd parted to avoid Joseph's hulking form. He walked ahead of me, his big body shielding mine. I squeezed his hand tighter, and his thumb rubbed across my palm in a reassuring caress.

Out of the corner of my eye, I saw Jayme just before we stepped outside. She barely paused her carefree dancing to give me a thumbs-up. She'd been so deep in the crowd that I doubted she'd seen what'd happened with Stu. My bestie would've come to my rescue alongside Joseph. And she'd have a lot more questions about my decision to leave with the gorgeous bartender so early in the evening if she'd seen the scuffle.

As it was, Jayme had no inkling that Stu had freaked me out, and she was simply happy to see me holding hands with Joseph. I suspected she wouldn't be coming back to our apartment for a while, granting me plenty of alone-time with my crush.

Now that he was actually going to take me home after weeks of sexual tension building between us, it seemed surreal. I'd second-guessed his interest in me so many times, but there was no longer any doubt in my mind. Joseph wanted me.

Chapter Three
JOSEPH

There was no going back now. When that entitled asshole put his hands on her, I hadn't been able to restrain my more violent urges. And by the time she placed her hand in mine, trusting me to protect her and take her home, her fate was sealed.

"Do you want to get an Uber?" she asked when we stepped out into the crisp autumn air.

I finally turned to look at her, and any lingering doubt left my mind. I didn't give a fuck about the complications that might keep her from me. For tonight, she was mine. I'd be a gentleman and take her home, but I'd steal a goodnight kiss, at the very least. If she invited me in after that, I wouldn't hold anything back. I wouldn't be able to, not after weeks of fantasizing about her soft body pinned beneath mine.

"I'll drive," I said, realizing I'd waited a second too long to answer. Her flushed cheeks and sparkling sapphire eyes were very distracting. I'd only ever seen her in the dim lighting of the bar, but now her ivory skin was illuminated by the streetlights. She practically shined, every bit the angel I'd envisioned.

"Okay," she agreed, seemingly unconcerned at the prospect of getting in the car with a near-stranger. I should've pointed out that her decision-making could put her at risk with another man, but I didn't want to spook her. So I said nothing, swallowing the urge to correct her.

There were other, darker ways I'd like to reprimand her. More times than I could count, I'd envisioned the way her shapely ass would bounce beneath my hand as I spanked her.

But she was far too pure and perfect to be subjected to such perversions. For her, I could hold back that particularly savage part of myself. I'd spare her from the worst of my animal urges.

That didn't mean I wasn't going to touch her.

I allowed her to catch up a step, and when she was within reach, I placed my hand at the small of her back. She didn't protest. Instead, a light shiver raced through her body.

"Are you cold?" I asked.

"Y-yes," she stuttered slightly, and I suspected she wasn't simply chilled from the cool night air. "Um, I'm still not used to this weather. I'm a Georgia girl."

"What year are you?"

Please don't say freshman. If she was eighteen or under, I couldn't justify fucking her. Not if she was more than five years younger than me.

"Sophomore," she replied. "This is my second year at Harvard, but I don't think I'll ever get used to the cold."

I took the invitation to wrap my arm around her waist, pulling her closer to my body heat. She leaned into me, tucking herself against my side like she belonged there.

I couldn't hold back the satisfied smile that twisted my lips.

"You should wear a jacket," I admonished, although I was grateful for the excuse to hold her.

"I wear about five layers or more to class, but I don't like to wear a coat to the bar. I don't want to lose it. I usually jump in and out of an Uber, so it's not too bad."

I didn't say it aloud, but I'd appreciated her more form-fitting dresses many times. I didn't at all mind that she decided to forgo her multiple layers.

We arrived at my car—a beaten-up black Corolla

I'd bought in cash from a more unscrupulous dealer. I hadn't wanted the purchase to be traced back to me. Every move I'd made since relocating to Cambridge had been calculated to cover my tracks.

I'd been careful. It was highly unlikely that anyone would find me. The risk to Ashlyn was minimal. And even on the slim chance that a threat did arise, I could protect her.

My chest swelled as she pressed herself even closer to my side, trusting me completely. I'd defended her from that creep in the bar, and it'd felt damn good to unleash my violent instincts to protect rather than to punish. Especially when Ashlyn stared at me with those big blue eyes like I was some kind of fucking hero.

With every passing second, her nearness intoxicated me, and it was becoming easier to convince myself that I could claim her. That I *should* claim her.

That fucker who'd put his hands on her might not leave her alone, no matter what I'd threatened. It would be better for her if I was around to keep her safe.

My resolve firmed as I guided her to the passenger side and opened the door for her, taking her hand as she slid into the seat. Unwilling to break physical contact so soon, I leaned in and buckled her seatbelt, allowing my hands to linger around her body for a few seconds longer than necessary.

"I can get it," she protested, but her breathing hitched.

"You could," I allowed, smirking with satisfaction. She hadn't batted my hands away, and her protest had been husky with desire.

I was definitely getting that goodnight kiss.

"You sure you're okay?" I asked when I got into the driver's seat. I glanced over at her, assessing. The streetlight caught in her lovely eyes, making them shine like gemstones.

"What? Oh, yeah. The Stu thing. I'm fine."

Stu. I'd known for weeks that the bastard was interested in Ashlyn. I'd seen how he watched her, how he leaned in close when he talked to her. I hadn't liked it, but she hadn't been mine. I couldn't stop other men from hitting on her when I had no claim over her.

But when he put his hands on her, all that had changed. The violence that brewed within me—the savage instincts I'd tried so hard to deny—had risen up with blinding force. It'd taken all my willpower to stop myself from smashing my fist into his nose and ruining his pretty-boy face.

"Thanks," she said. Her dainty hand covered mine. "You didn't have to defend me like that."

"Yes, I did." I couldn't have stood back and watched him touch her. She was too pure for his taint.

I turned my hand so that our palms touched, and I laced my fingers through hers. Although her hand was so much smaller, it fit perfectly in my careful grip.

"Where do you live?" I asked. "I'll take you home."

"Towne Apartments. Thanks."

"You don't have to keep thanking me. I'm happy to do it."

"Oh. Sorry."

One corner of my mouth ticked up. She really was adorable. "You don't have to apologize, either."

Her hand tensed in mine, and I knew she was feeling awkward. I'd watched her often from across the bar, noticing how she'd stiffen with anxiety and fiddle with her fingernails when boys talked to her.

I wasn't a *boy*, and I definitely didn't want to make her nervous.

Not in that way, at least.

The familiar fantasy of Ashlyn trembling beneath my touch flashed across my mind, and I barely managed to keep my fingers gentle on hers.

"Relax," I urged. "You're safe with me."

I heard her take a breath, and the tension drained from her body. I kept my hold on her hand as I drove the short distance to her apartment. The silence that filled the car wasn't uncomfortable; it was thick with sensual tension, and I didn't dare break it with an inane question about her studies. Besides, I didn't want her asking too many questions about my life. I'd resolved to put my dark past behind me, and that meant hiding it from everyone in my new life, even her.

Especially her.

I'd never experienced such a strong physical connection to any woman, and the long weeks of denial had only intensified the feeling. If we'd shared a quick fuck on the night I'd first laid eyes on her, maybe I could've gotten her out of my system. As it was, I idolized her. In my mind, I'd made her into more than just another beautiful woman. She was the life I craved, everything I couldn't have and didn't deserve.

Tonight, I'd finally get a taste of what I so desperately wanted.

I parked outside her apartment complex and got out to open the car door for her. She was already halfway on her feet by the time I got to her, but I took her hand again, as though she needed my help. A stupid, delusional part of me was enjoying playing the part of her white knight. I'd protected her from Stu.

I'd do my best to protect her from the darker parts of myself, too. I owed her at least that much.

She didn't pull her hand from mine when I closed the car door behind her.

"I'll walk you to your door." I was going to see her safely into her apartment, and I would taste her lips before I left.

She glanced up at me and licked those lush, pink lips. My cock throbbed in response to the sign of desire.

"Okay," she agreed softly. "My place is this way."

She started walking toward the brick porch that lined the front of the fancy townhouses. I kept step beside her, still holding her hand in mine.

We arrived at one of the ten identical units, and she retrieved her keys from her purse. When she unlocked the door, I squeezed her fingers lightly, calling her full attention back to me. Her sapphire gaze caught mine, and her pouty lips parted on a little sigh.

"Thanks for bringing me home. You didn't have to—"

"Yes, I did," I interrupted her. I hadn't had a choice. Not once Stu put his hands on her. I wouldn't have been capable of working the rest of my shift at the bar. I wouldn't have been capable of thinking about anything but branding her with my touch, erasing the taint where he'd grabbed her.

Unable to hold back, I reached out and caressed her cheek, relishing the softness of her skin beneath my fingertips. She didn't flinch away from the intimate contact; she tilted her face into my hand, welcoming more. I slid my fingers into her dark, silken hair and hooked my thumb beneath her jaw, capturing her. Her soft intake of breath went straight to my cock, and I closed the distance between us with a hungry growl.

I didn't take her lips with the tender care she deserved. I crushed my mouth to hers, and she opened for me on a sharp, shocked gasp.

She didn't shrink from my sudden aggression. Her arms twined around the back of my neck, and she pulled me closer as she pressed her soft body against mine. Lust ignited my system, pulsing through me with visceral intensity I'd never known before. My fingers tightened in her hair, tugging the silky strands and tipping her head back so I could take her mouth more deeply. My tongue swept inside to glide against hers. She tasted like the fruity cocktail she'd sipped at the bar and something darker, more delicious. Her body melted into mine, softening and heating as she molded herself against me. I wrapped one arm around her waist, pulling her impossibly closer. She shivered in my hold, but it wasn't the chilly night air that elicited the response. The heat between us was too intense for the cold to touch either of us.

When we were both desperate for air, I finally released her mouth. She stared up at me, breathing hard. Her pupils were dilated, the sapphire ring of her irises narrowing as her eyes darkened with lust.

"Do you want to come inside?" she asked breathlessly.

More than anything. Instead of making the intimate admission, I nodded.

She turned from me and fumbled at the doorknob, her hand trembling from the keen desire that tormented us both. I reached around her and closed my fingers over hers, firmly turning the knob and pushing the door open. Now that I'd held her in my arms, I couldn't wait to feel her lush body pressed up against mine again.

When I closed the door behind us, she took my hand in hers and led me toward her bedroom. I hadn't expected such boldness from her, but the raw need that drove both of us to a frenzy was stronger than the anxiety I'd sensed in her earlier.

I was curious to check out the way she chose to decorate her room—to understand her personality better. But in that moment, I was far more curious to learn other things about her. Like the sounds she'd make when I kissed her neck and caressed her breasts.

I leaned in to take her lips again, but she pulled back slightly. In the dim lighting that illuminated the bedroom through the shades, I could see that she'd lowered her lashes in shyness.

"I, um, I don't want to have sex. Not tonight," she said quietly. "I don't want to give you the wrong impression."

Even though it made my balls ache to hear it, I wasn't surprised. I'd been right to think Ashlyn was innocent. She wasn't the type to take a near-stranger home and fuck him. I'd never met a woman who didn't eagerly fall into bed with me. The chase, the challenge, only deepened my fascination with her.

I curled two fingers beneath her chin and lifted her face to mine.

"No sex," I agreed. "I wouldn't have hoped for anything more than a goodnight kiss. Thank you for trusting me and inviting me in."

Before her shyness could return, I captured her lips again. Her soft moan made my cock throb, and I savored the way the little sound vibrated against my tongue as I stroked into her mouth. Never releasing her, I moved toward the shadowed outline of her bed and guided her down onto her back. I settled my weight over her on instinct, craving to feel her small body pinned beneath mine.

She stiffened for a moment, and I knew she must feel overpowered, trapped.

My cock jerked again, but I pulled my lips from hers so I could reassure her.

"I'm not going to do anything you're not comfortable with," I promised her. "If you want me to stop—or even leave—just say the word. You're in control here."

Those last words felt wrong on my tongue. I wanted to dominate her, to hear her beg and whimper my name. But I would never violate an unwilling woman, and I certainly wouldn't subject Ashlyn to those darker fantasies.

She licked her plush lips and gave me a little nod, letting me know she wanted me to continue.

"Good girl," I rumbled without thinking. It felt right to praise her this way, to guide and encourage her to release the more sensual side of herself.

I leaned in and kissed her neck at the little hollow beneath her ear. She gasped and shuddered. I licked at her sensitive skin, tasting her sweet flavor and relishing her every panting breath. She arched up into me, her breasts pressing against my chest as her short fingernails bit into the back of my neck. She drew me closer, silently begging for more.

I growled and nipped at her shoulder. She let out a soft cry. Despite the desire in the sound, I reined myself in. I couldn't mark her with my teeth as I wanted to. I wouldn't mar the smooth perfection of her skin with my bite.

Aching to explore her curves, I reached between us and cupped her breast. I could feel her peaked nipple through her dress, and I realized she wasn't wearing a bra. I groaned into her mouth, loving the shape and feel of her lush body. Her moan mingled with my sound of pleasure, and she thrust her chest into my touch.

I played with her like that for a long time, learning her body and her sensual triggers. She writhed and moaned beneath me, clinging to me as I teased her and tasted her. I wanted to know everything about her. I wanted to know how hot and silky smooth her pussy would be if I touched her there. I could practically smell her desire, and I knew she was wet and welcoming.

Not tonight, I told myself. I'd promised her I wouldn't push for sex. I'd honor the trust she'd shown me.

"Please," she said on a throaty groan. "Please, Joseph." She rocked her hips against my thigh, seeking stimulation.

The sound of her husky voice caressing my name

as she begged for my touch cracked some of my resolve.

"You want to come, angel?" I asked, using the endearment without realizing.

"I...I need..." She was too shy to ask for what she wanted.

"I have to hear you say it. I need your consent."

I need to hear you beg. I need to hear the dirty words falling from your sweet lips.

"Please touch me."

I eased one hand beneath the hem of her dress, gliding my palm up her thigh. Her skin was even softer than I'd imagined, and I bit back a growl of desire as my dick throbbed.

When I reached her wet heat, I teased my fingers along the edge of her lace panties.

"Touch you, where?" I prompted. "Here?" I brushed my thumb across her clit through the barrier of the lace, and she cried out.

"Yes!"

"Say it," I commanded, unable to hold back my more domineering nature now that I had her squirming and begging. "Ask me to touch your pretty pussy."

She hesitated, her embarrassment creeping back. I found her innocence delicious, but I found corrupting that innocence even more appealing.

I withdrew my hand, silently communicating that she wouldn't get the reward she wanted until she obeyed.

"Wait! Please, Joseph. Please touch my..."

I waited, refusing to cave until she gave me what I wanted.

"Please touch my pussy." It was barely more than a whisper, but the words went straight to my head, suffusing me with power that was even more intoxicating than my physical desire for her.

I took her lips again, my chest rumbling with pleasure as I dipped my fingers beneath her panties. She was just as hot and silky soft as I'd hoped: wet and ready for me. I longed to get inside her, to fuck her and brand her with my own heat.

But I'd made a promise, and I'd never betray her sweet trust in me.

I circled her clit with my thumb, teasing around it. Even the light touch elicited a harsh shout from her, and I caught the sound of her pleasure on my tongue. All it took was a direct, firm touch to her clit, and she came undone. She tensed beneath me, and her fingers curled into my upper arms as she clung on tight. She screamed out her ecstasy, and I smothered the sound with a rough, possessive kiss.

I stroked her for a few seconds longer, withdrawing my hand when she began to shudder. She would be sensitive after such a powerful orgasm, and I didn't want to torment her. Not this first time, anyway.

I finally released her lips, and she stared up at me, breathing hard. She reached between us, and her fingers brushed my rock-hard cock through my jeans.

I swallowed a curse and grasped her wrist, directing her touch away from my aching dick.

"No," I refused. "Not tonight."

"But what about you?"

"I'll be okay," I promised, although my gut was knotted with tension. I didn't want her to do anything she'd regret in the morning. I never wanted her to regret spending this night with me.

"Come here," I urged, rolling off her and positioning myself on my side. I pulled her body against mine, and she tucked her face into my neck with a contented little sigh. The sound eased some of the knots in my stomach, and my lust subsided a little.

I kissed the top of her head, and she began to breathe deeply, falling asleep quickly after her orgasm.

I lay awake for a long time after, relishing the feel of her in my arms. I was still hard for her when I finally drifted into sleep.

I woke up before Ashlyn the following morning. In the light of dawn, the possessive haze that'd descended on my mind the night before began to clear.

I wasn't some fucking hero, no matter how Ashlyn's wide eyes had shined when she placed her hand in mine. She'd looked to me for protection, but she'd been shaken after her encounter with that handsy asshole. If I hadn't been the one to force Stu away from her, she might've been rescued by some other, more noble guy. She never would've had reason to allow me to escort her home.

I should've had more self-control. I shouldn't have been a fucking idiot and deluded myself into thinking that I was actually *good* for her.

I knew I should leave. I should go to my shithole apartment, gather my few belongings, and get out of Cambridge. I should leave her behind so that no one from my old, violent life could threaten her because of me.

But then she opened her lovely eyes, and I knew I couldn't do it. Her soft, sleepy smile pierced my chest and hooked somewhere deep inside me, tethering me to her.

"Hi," she said, her voice raspy from sleep. The husky tone went straight to my cock, and I took a breath to suppress my lust.

A crooked smile curved my lips, and I tucked a stray lock of dark hair behind her ear, caressing her face as though I had every right to touch her so casually. "Hi. Sleep well?"

She breathed out a happy sigh and pressed her cheek against my chest. "Wonderfully, thanks." She wrapped her arms around me and snuggled in, as though she couldn't stop clinging to me.

I knew the feeling. I held her closer, relishing her soft, floral scent.

She curved her leg over my hip, and my cock throbbed. I gritted my teeth and forced myself to pull away from her.

"I have to go," I told her, pain roughening each forced word.

Her eyes clouded, confusion and a touch of hurt darkening their blue depths.

"Oh. Will I see you later?" Some of her shyness returned, softening her tone to little more than a whisper.

"Of course," I heard myself say before I could stop the promise from leaving my lips. When she looked at me like that—needy and achingly vulnerable—I couldn't refuse her. I couldn't bring myself to hurt her.

And truthfully, I didn't want to bear the pain of leaving her.

I pressed a kiss against her forehead. If I couldn't do the honorable thing and leave her alone, I'd at least treat her like she deserved. "I'll take you out to dinner. I'll pick you up tonight."

After a few more lingering kisses, I managed to pry myself away from her so she could get ready for class.

Although guilt twisted my gut, the unpleasant sensation couldn't dull the warm, hopeful glow in my chest. Maybe I could lead a normal life here. Maybe Ashlyn could be mine.

Chapter Four
JOSEPH

The late afternoon shift at the bar was predictably slow. I didn't understand why the managers bothered opening before ten PM. That was when the students started arriving.

As it was, I'd spent the last four hours deep cleaning the place, since there weren't any customers in sight. After I'd abandoned my shift last night to be with Ashlyn, my coworker Sara hadn't done the best job at cleanup.

I didn't blame her. I'd kind of fucked her over, leaving without so much as an apology.

So, I scrubbed the bar, grateful for the distraction from my conflicted thoughts about pulling Ashlyn into my life.

Before I'd escaped to Cambridge, I'd never so much as wiped down a counter in my own home.

We'd had half a dozen household staff who handled mundane chores.

But now, I didn't mind the work. I'd scrub floors for the rest of my life and live in a shitty studio apartment if it meant that I could be free from my old life, my *family*.

When my short, solo shift ended, Sara arrived to take over. She glared at me, but she didn't rip me a new one for abandoning her. She accepted my apology with a tight nod and a dismissive wave for me to leave. Grateful that she seemed willing to move past it, I left the bar without trying harder to make amends. I got the feeling Sara would rather not have me in her space today. At least she hadn't called our manager to get me fired. If I wasn't going to leave town, I needed this job.

When I stepped out of the bar into the twilight, my senses immediately went on high alert. The parking lot was empty except for my Corolla and Sara's Buick, but I wasn't alone out here. I'd spent years stalking people, intimidating them. I knew what it felt like to be watched, hunted.

If my family had tracked me down—or worse, my family's enemies—I had to get out of town and get away from Ashlyn.

But I wasn't going to leave her unless I was sure.

I decided she was worth the risk.

I reached into my pocket and pulled out the cheap burner phone I'd bought when I first arrived in Cambridge. I'd keep the call short, and then I'd ditch the phone.

I entered the number I knew by heart and connected the call. It rang three times before the familiar, clipped voice sounded through the line.

"Who the fuck is this?"

"Are you following me?" I asked immediately, not willing to spend a second longer on the phone than necessary.

A beat of stunned silence passed. "Joseph?"

"I asked you a question, Marco," I growled. "Are you following me? Do you have people looking for me?"

"Of course I have people looking for you. Where the fuck are you?"

I cursed and ended the call. Marco wouldn't lie to me. I wasn't surprised that my best friend had people searching for me, but if he truly hadn't discovered my location, then that meant someone else was watching me. And they weren't part of my own family. While I didn't want anyone to find me, allies would have been preferable to enemies.

I threw the phone down onto the pavement. It shattered, and I finished crushing it under my boot. I wouldn't be able to keep that number. Not after calling Marco.

"If I had that piece of shit phone, I'd smash it too."

I whirled and found Stu approaching me, flanked by two of his preppy-boy lackeys.

Fuck. I'd jeopardized my hideout because of this asshole?

Even as relief washed through me, my fists curled at my sides. I'd put my location at risk by calling Marco, and it was Stu's fault.

"What the fuck do you want?" I snapped, but it was pretty clear what they were here for.

They wanted to beat the shit out of me. I'd embarrassed Stu in front of dozens of his classmates, and he couldn't let that slide. I understood his need to save face, but I wasn't interested in getting involved in this pissing contest. I'd seen enough violence to last a lifetime, and I didn't feel like kicking his teeth in. He'd touched Ashlyn, but he'd paid for that when I publicly humiliated him last night.

"I want to kick your townie ass," Stu sneered.

So, he was an elitist dick as well as a misogynistic asshole. Great.

"Fine." I shrugged out of my leather jacket and tossed it aside. It would only get in the way. "You and me. Let's go." I sneered at him to rile his pride. "Or are you such a chickenshit that you need your boys to back you up?" I could take all three of them if I had to, but I didn't want to resort to that level of brutality.

Stu swallowed and swayed back a bit, but his expression quickly hardened with determination. He handed his own jacket off to one of his friends, his movements slightly jerky with tense apprehension.

"Okay. You and me, you townie piece of shit."

Back home, no one would've dared to talk to me that way. And I couldn't deny that the insult stung a little. I'd much rather be a normal college student, but that life had been denied me.

I wasn't about to show this asshole any weakness, though. I simply stared at him coolly and waited for him to come to me. He hesitated, clearly unnerved by my calm demeanor. I could tell he wasn't used to fighting. Not like I was. Fighting was in my past, in my blood. I'd been trying to escape from the relentless violence of my life, but I would call on my more ruthless skills to defend myself from this prick. He deserved to have his ass kicked, anyway. He'd touched Ashlyn. That was enough to make me see red.

Stu came at me with a wild, sloppy swing. I dodged easily and moved in close to slam my fist into his gut. He dropped to one knee, wheezing.

Unfortunately, his friends weren't willing to let me finish him off that easily. Before I could ask if Stu had taken enough, one of his lackey's fists connected with my jaw.

Fuck. I should've been paying more attention. I was rusty, going soft after months of separation from my old life.

I reeled back, and before I could get my bearings, another hit rattled my ribcage.

The pain sharpened my focus rather than distracting me, and I moved with brutal precision. Stu was still down on his knees. I turned on the bigger of the two men that were still attacking. He was barely more than a boy, really. I almost felt bad when I broke his nose.

Almost.

He fell to the asphalt, clutching at his face and groaning. I turned to my last opponent, only to see him sprinting off across the parking lot, fleeing from me.

Smart guy.

I rubbed my aching jaw and winced at the contact. That was going to bruise, and I had my date with Ashlyn in a few hours. I considered kicking Stu for that, but I wouldn't beat a man who was already down.

I'd be damned if I painted my hands with more

blood because of this bastard. Not when those hands would touch Ashlyn. I wouldn't allow that taint to mar her purity and innocence.

"Are we done here?" I asked coldly.

Stu nodded without meeting my eyes, unable to draw enough breath to form words. His friend was still moaning on the ground beside him.

"I don't want to see your face again," I told him. "Don't come back here."

He managed another nod, and I decided I was satisfied with his defeat. I didn't have to hurt him more to make my point. The whole "fight" had lasted less than five minutes. I was pretty sure they understood that they couldn't fuck with me.

I picked up my jacket and calmly walked to my car. Stu and his friend were still down when I pulled out of the parking lot.

I pushed them from my mind and chose to ignore the pain in my jaw and side. I'd dealt with much worse.

Besides, it was easy to forget about the discomfort when I had my date with Ashlyn to look forward to.

Chapter Five
ASHLYN

My heart stuttered when I opened the door to reveal Joseph waiting on my front porch. His aquamarine eyes and cocky smile were as striking as ever, but they weren't what caught my attention. A bruise darkened his jaw, marring his beauty with signs of violence.

"Oh my god," I exclaimed. "What happened?" I reached out to brush my fingers across the mark, careful not to apply pressure.

He shrugged. "It's nothing. I'm fine."

"That's not what I asked," I clarified. "I'm glad you feel fine, but I asked you what happened."

He blinked at me, then grinned.

"What?" I demanded, not understanding his levity. He was hurt, and he was acting like it was nothing.

"You're not as shy as I thought," he said, amusement coloring his tone.

My cheeks heated. It wasn't like me to be so assertive, but social awkwardness was one thing. Concern for his wellbeing was another.

I lifted my chin. "Are you going to tell me what happened, or not?"

He chuckled. "Just a little misunderstanding with Stu."

My brows shot up. "A misunderstanding?" I hoped this wasn't about me, but I wasn't vain enough to ask that.

Joseph nodded. "Stu thought he and his bros could beat me up. They were mistaken."

I softened. "But you're hurt. Do you need to see a doctor or something?"

His grin widened. "For this? I've had much worse. Like I said, I'm fine." He reached out and took my hand in his. "I'd feel a lot better if you'd let me take you to dinner, though."

"But why did they try to beat you up?" I asked, even as I allowed him to lead me toward his car.

He glanced down at me. "Do you really have to ask?"

I blushed and cut my eyes away. I couldn't believe men had fought over me. It was strange, and more than a little disconcerting.

"I'm sorry you got hurt because of me."

He squeezed my hand gently, pulling my gaze back to his. "It wasn't your fault. Stu chose to get angry. He made a stupid decision to try to save face after I embarrassed him at the bar. Besides, I'm barely bruised. I'm okay, really."

I gaped at him. How could he say that? I knew some men got into fights occasionally, but I wasn't accustomed to casual violence.

I decided not to press him on it. Maybe he was putting on a brave front, and I didn't want to damage his ego by fussing over him. If he wanted to be all macho about defending my honor, I wouldn't make him feel bad about it. In fact, it was kind of hot. I wasn't happy that he'd been hurt, of course, but the idea of Joseph as my knight in shining armor was undeniably swoon-worthy.

He ushered me to his car and opened the door for me, like a gentleman. The way his hands lingered around my body when he buckled my seatbelt wasn't as gentlemanly. My pulse raced in response to his nearness.

Too soon, he drew away and took his place on the driver's side. He held my hand in his as he drove. The contact was casual, familiar; as though we'd done this hundreds of times. Being with him, having him touch me, felt as natural as breathing.

To my surprise, we pulled into the parking lot of one of the nicest Italian restaurants in town. Delrio's was known for its delicious—but expensive—Sicilian dishes, and even the wealthier students at Harvard didn't make a habit of splurging there regularly.

"Is this okay?" Joseph asked as he helped me out of the car.

"You didn't have to bring me here." He didn't need to throw money around to impress me, and I didn't like thinking that he'd spend all his tips for the week on one dinner date with me.

"They serve the best food in town," he countered, waving away my concern. "I wanted to bring you here."

"Thank you." I wasn't really sure what else to say. I didn't want to offend him by bringing up his salary, but I still wasn't entirely comfortable with the extravagance of the venue. "I think I'm underdressed," I said to cover the real reason for my tension.

Truthfully, it was a genuine concern. I'd put on a pretty, lavender cashmere sweater, but I really should be wearing a dress rather than jeans.

He smiled down at me as he opened the restaurant door. "You'll be the most beautiful woman here. No one will care what you're wearing."

I flushed, but I couldn't drop my eyes from his

burning, flame-blue gaze. No man had ever looked at me the way Joseph did: like he worshipped me but wanted to devour me at the same time.

"You look nice, too," I finally managed. He was even more dressed-down than I was, wearing his usual black shirt, leather jacket, dark jeans, and heavy black boots. But he was beautiful enough that he could easily be a model or movie star. No one would turn Joseph away from any venue, no matter what he was wearing.

His lips curved with pleasure and a hint of amusement. "Thank you."

Our intimate moment was shattered when a pretty blonde server showed us to our table. Joseph didn't so much as glance in her direction. It was as though he was transfixed by me, his full attention keen to the point that it should've been uncomfortable.

I reveled in it, basking in the warm glow of his overt admiration. Not only was it an ego boost, but no one in my life—romantically involved or otherwise—had ever considered me with such rapt interest, as though they were trying to peer straight into my soul. It made me feel powerful and achingly vulnerable at the same time, and I was quickly becoming addicted to the sensation.

When we got to our table, Joseph pulled out my chair for me. His gentlemanly behavior was at odds with his bad-boy sense of style, and the combination was enticing. I was definitely becoming infatuated far too quickly. But if I was honest with myself, I'd been a goner the moment our eyes first met across the bar all those weeks ago.

Joseph ordered a glass of champagne for each of us, and the waitress didn't even glance at me to assess my age. She only had eyes for Joseph, so she quickly nodded and rushed off to fulfill his order. It should've made me jealous, but the fact that he was still fully focused on me mollified any resentment I might have felt.

"You didn't have to get me champagne," I said, still worried about the extravagance of the evening.

He fixed me with a suddenly stern stare. "You keep telling me what I don't have to do. I know I don't have to. I want to do these things for you."

"Oh." I hadn't thought about it that way. I'd been feeling guilty every time he did something nice for me. I wasn't accustomed to being treated with such care and attention. "Thank you. I guess I'm just not used to it, is all."

His head canted to the side. "You're not used to people being nice to you?"

I shifted in my seat. This was a deeper question than I'd anticipated. I really liked Joseph, but I wasn't ready to trust so easily. No matter how badly I wanted to.

"I'm just not used to so much attention, I guess."

His dark brows lifted. "You can't tell me that men don't fall at your feet all the time."

I practically squirmed in my chair, uncomfortable with such intense scrutiny. "I guess I just don't spend that much time with boys."

He considered me for a moment, then nodded. "Well, I'm not a *boy*. I want to treat you how you deserve to be treated. You need to let me."

The last held the ring of command, but it didn't bother me. If anything, his unyielding tone made it easier for me to agree. I could let go of my social anxiety and allow him to take care of me in the way he wanted.

"All right." The agreement left my lips without a thought of protest.

His dazzling grin hit me square in the chest, and I almost forgot how to breathe. "Good girl."

That seemed like an odd thing to say, but the words made something heat low in my belly.

"I'm not a girl," I managed to say, although there wasn't any fire behind the assertion.

His gaze blazed again, the candlelight catching in his pale blue eyes. "No, you're not. Does it bother you that I said it?"

I considered for a moment, then decided to tell the truth. "No."

His cocky smile returned. "Excellent."

I didn't understand why he seemed so pleased with my response, but his levity was catching, and I found myself grinning like a fool.

Our champagne arrived, and Joseph ordered our meal without even glancing at the menu.

When the waitress left, he focused on me. "I hope you don't mind that I ordered for both of us. This is my favorite cuisine, and I want you to try a few things."

"I don't mind," I assured him, and I really didn't. The feminist in me should probably be annoyed, but I liked that he wanted to share something he enjoyed with me. I craved to know more about him. "Have you been to Delrio's before, then?"

"A few times. My family owns a similar restaurant back home, and the food here is almost as good."

I leaned forward, latching on to the first real thing I'd learned about him. "Your family owns a restaurant? Where?"

His expression shuttered, closing him off from me. "New York."

"Oh. So that's home for you?" I fiddled with my napkin in my lap, my anxiety returning with his sudden distance.

"Not anymore." He blew out a heavy breath, and his smile returned. "I like living in Cambridge."

"What's your favorite thing about living here?" I asked quickly, relieved that his tension had passed.

He studied me with fresh hunger. "I should think that would be obvious. I got to meet you."

My breath caught in my throat. It was a startlingly intense thing to say, but it made my pulse race.

"I'm glad I met you, too," I said.

He reached out and picked up his champagne glass, raising it for a toast. I mirrored his movement and touched my glass to his.

"Cheers," he said simply, but the toast felt much heavier than the lighthearted sentiment. We were drinking to celebrate the fact that we'd met.

I tipped my glass back and allowed a generous sip of the bubbly drink to fizz over my tongue. I was savoring more than the decadent flavor; I was relishing this moment with him. It seemed surreal that just last night, I'd doubted his interest in me. Already, I felt more bonded to him than I had to any other man, and we'd barely shared anything about ourselves. I wanted to know more about him, but he spoke first.

"Tell me about your studies." Again, it wasn't exactly a question, and again, I didn't mind. I kind of liked how direct he was. It was refreshing and sexy.

"I'm an Art History major. I just declared this semester. My dad wanted me to study Psychology like him, but I wasn't really passionate about it."

His eyes sparkled with something like yearning. "I'd love to study a subject like Art History. That's amazing."

"Are you into art?"

He shrugged. "I've studied it a little. I've studied a little of everything. It's more the idea of it that I like. You're not choosing the practical route, but you're following your passion. That's very brave of you. Not many people make that kind of choice."

The compliment warmed me all the way to my toes. I'd never thought of it that way. In fact, I'd worried that I was making a foolish choice. My father certainly thought so.

"Thank you," I said. "What was your major?"

His expression went carefully blank again, and my stomach dropped. I'd touched on a tense subject again without meaning to.

"I didn't go to college. I wanted to, but I didn't get the opportunity. It's one of the reasons I moved to Cambridge. I wanted to see what it was like, living in a college town." His gaze turned inward. "Sometimes, I think I'm torturing myself."

I was sure he hadn't intended to say that last part aloud.

I reached out and covered his hand with mine, calling his attention back to me. I didn't know if finances had prevented him from attending college or something else, but I wasn't going to press him about it. It clearly was a sore subject for him, and I didn't want to ruin the evening.

"Well, I'm glad you moved here," I said fervently. "Really glad."

His smile returned, and relief washed through me. He turned his hand so that his palm pressed against mine, and his thumb caressed my fingers. "Me too."

The rest of dinner was more lighthearted. Joseph shared his favorite dishes with me, occasionally feeding me from his plate. It was strange and intense and incredibly sensual.

By the time we finished dessert, I was still hungry, but not for food.

"Do you want to come back to my place?" I asked when we were back in the privacy of his car. "Not just to drop me off, I mean."

"I'd love that. Thank you."

His gratitude warmed my insides. He wasn't

taking my offer for granted; he hadn't expected to buy my affection with a fancy meal.

But I was more than ready to give him what we both so desperately wanted. It wasn't at all like me to fall into bed so quickly, but with Joseph, I couldn't hold back. I didn't want to.

Chapter Six
ASHLYN

Joseph's kiss was scorching, branding. Every kiss before his had been a fumbling, passionless affair. I'd never known what I was missing until our lips touched for the first time. He was harsh and demanding, but he held me with reverence even as his mouth subjugated mine. I felt cherished and utterly consumed at the same time, and I knew he felt the same desperate need that tormented me.

We moved through my apartment and into my bedroom in a frenzy, and by the time we closed the door behind us, my sweater had already been stripped off and tossed aside.

"Turn on the light," he said, low and rough. "I want to see you."

A delighted flush heated my skin, and I did as he

commanded. I wanted to see him, too. I'd felt his hard body while we'd made out the night before, but we hadn't been naked together.

Even though I didn't usually strip down around men, I wasn't self-conscious about my body. I put in enough hours swimming laps every week that I was used to my curves being on display in my bathing suit.

This was different, though. Because Joseph was watching me like a starving man at a feast, and I was still covered by my jeans and bra.

He began to touch me with shockingly gentle hands, his slow, reverent movements in contrast to how he'd been kissing me so roughly. His fingertips skimmed around my waist before coming up behind my back to unhook my simple black bra. He slid the straps down my arms, his eyes fixed on my chest as he slowly revealed my breasts. His jaw clenched. I got the feeling he was holding himself back, savoring the sight of me instead of pinning me down and kissing me the way he had last night.

I shivered as cool air caressed my heated skin, and my nipples pebbled to hard peaks. He ran his knuckles over the needy buds. I gasped and arched into his touch, craving more.

A rumbling sound of pleasure left his chest, and he cupped my breasts fully, his big hands completely encompassing them. His calloused palms teased against my nipples as he learned the weight and shape of my breasts, still touching me with aching care.

"Joseph, please." I needed more. I leaned into him and clutched at his upper arms.

He withdrew, and I whined my protest.

"Shhh," he urged. "I'm not finished."

His long fingers trailed down my abdomen, teasing along the top of my jeans before he deftly freed the button at the front. He pulled down the zipper in a torturously slow motion, but I didn't beg for him to go faster. I craved more contact, but the way he studied me with such rapt fascination was addictive.

He finally hooked his thumbs through the top of my jeans and my panties, and he pulled them down my legs. He dropped to his knees before me, his eyes riveted on my sex as I compliantly stepped out of my jeans and flats.

He simply stared for several seconds. I shifted on my feet, but not out of anxiety; it was all I could do to stop myself from rocking my hips toward his lips in wanton invitation.

He leaned in, close enough that his hot breath teased across my clit. Without thinking, I spread my legs, craving his touch. He pressed a soft, sweet kiss just above my clit.

"Beautiful." The word vibrated against my flesh as his lips brushed my skin.

"Please," I begged again.

He shot me a wicked grin, his eyes lifting to meet mine. "You want me to kiss your pretty pussy, angel?"

Angel. He'd called me that once before. It only made me feel more worshipped, and I fell deeper into his thrall, intoxicated by his reverence for me.

I licked my lips. I did want him to put his mouth on me, but there was something I craved even more.

"I want to see you too."

I grasped his arms and guided him back to his feet. He allowed me to direct his movements; he was far too strong for me to physically force him to do anything he didn't want to do.

He nodded slightly, giving me permission to learn his body in the same way he'd explored mine.

I dipped my fingers beneath the hem of his tight black shirt, trailing my nails over his defined abs as I slowly lifted the cotton material. His muscles rippled and danced beneath my light touch, but he didn't try to hasten my movements.

When I'd raised his shirt enough to reveal his strong chest, he lifted it over his head, fully revealing his ripped torso. I wrapped my hands around his corded arms, loving the feel of his sculpted muscles.

I slid my hands downward, feeling his forearms

before shifting my touch to his jeans. I wasn't nearly as graceful as he'd been when he'd unbuttoned my pants. My fingers trembled from the intensity of the suppressed lust coursing through my system.

He didn't seem to mind. He remained perfectly still as I removed his jeans, feeling his powerful thighs as I stripped him. He toed off his boots and stepped out of his pants, leaving his body bare except for his boxers.

I hesitated, feeling suddenly shy. I could see the huge bulge of his erection straining against the cotton. It was intimidating, and I wasn't certain if I was bold enough to continue.

"You don't have to do anything you don't want to do." His tone was strained but deep with sincerity.

I glanced up at him and was immediately captured in his flame-blue gaze. His jaw ticked from the effort of holding himself back. He was fighting his animal urges for me; he didn't want to violate my trust.

That knowledge emboldened me. Never breaking eye contact with him, I tugged his boxers down, baring him completely, just as he'd done to me.

He allowed me to stare up at him in rapture for several long seconds.

"Look at me," he finally commanded.

I knew he wasn't ordering me to look him in the eye.

My gaze finally dropped to his cock, and I sucked in a sharp gasp. He was even bigger than I'd imagined, his thick erection straining toward me.

A desire to give him pleasure flooded me more strongly than any carnal need I'd ever known. My lips parted, and I leaned forward to take him into my mouth.

His fingers tangled in my hair, tugging me back.

"No," he bit out.

I glanced up at him, startled by his refusal. Before rejection could sting my heart, he explained himself.

"I don't want to come in your mouth. Not this time."

"Oh," I breathed. I realized I didn't want that, either. I wanted him inside me, stretching and filling me so we were connected in the most intimate way possible.

He bent down and grasped my waist in his strong hands, lifting me to my feet as though I weighed nothing. He guided me to the bed, settling his big body over me the way he'd done last night. I loved the heaviness of his muscular frame holding me down. It made me feel small and deliciously feminine, filling me with that strange mix of power and vulnerability.

I reached up and wrapped my arms around him, pulling him closer.

He hissed in a sharp breath. It wasn't a sound of pleasure.

I immediately withdrew my touch. "What's wrong?"

He shook his head. "It's nothing. I took a hit to my ribs earlier, but I'm fine. I'd just forgotten about it, is all." He gave me a crooked smile. "You're very distracting."

"I don't want to hurt you."

He cocked his head at me, considering for a moment. Then, something shifted in his eyes, and they darkened in a way I didn't fully understand.

"Put your hands over your head," he ordered.

I complied, not even thinking of protesting.

"Good girl. Keep them there. No matter what I do to you, keep them there."

"What are you going to do to me?" I asked, more intrigued than disconcerted by his command.

He dipped his head toward me, and his teeth grazed along the shell of my ear.

"Tease you. Torment you. Make you beg and scream my name." He sucked on my earlobe, nipping at it gently. "You'd like that, wouldn't you, angel? Tell me."

His words were heavier than simple dirty talk. He

needed my permission to continue with this game. I'd never engaged in anything remotely kinky, but I'd never been this hot and wet for a man in my life.

"Yes," I whispered. "I want it. I want you, Joseph."

He growled his savage approval, and the sound vibrated against my neck, making my sensitive skin spark and dance with awareness. I shivered and tilted my head to the side, exposing my throat to him.

I sucked in a sharp gasp when his palm settled over the front of my neck, his big hand nearly encircling it. He didn't apply any pressure, and to my surprise, fear didn't spike through me. Instead, lust flooded my system as I became fully aware of how small I was in his grip, the power he held over me. The domineering yet gentle way he handled me made my clit pulse, and wetness coated my thighs.

His thumb stroked the line of my vulnerable artery, and I shuddered. A husky groan left my chest, and I barely recognized that I'd made the sensual sound. I felt oddly light, disconnected from my normal self. With Joseph, I was freed from my anxiety and overactive brain. All I could focus on was *him*: his powerful body; his unique, masculine scent; the low, rumbling words of praise he uttered. He told me I was beautiful and perfect. His *angel*.

I became drunk on his attention, on the way he

worshipped my body even as he took full command of my entire being.

He stroked his fingers over my skin, as though he wanted to memorize my every curve. He kissed my breasts, pulling my nipples into his mouth and nipping at the sensitive buds. I began to writhe beneath him. I wanted to touch him, too, but I kept my arms securely over my head, obedient to his will.

"Please, please, please," I murmured over and over again in a desperate mantra. I needed him inside me. My pussy ached for him, and I was no longer afraid of his size. I craved to connect with him.

Finally, he brushed a kiss across my lips. "I'll be right back, angel."

He started to push off me, but I didn't want him to put even an inch of space between us. I was too enraptured by the feel of his weight pinning me down.

"No!" I protested, a little wildly.

"I need to get a condom," he explained, but his face was tight with his own need. He didn't want to leave me, either. Not even for a minute.

I forced myself to nod my agreement. A condom was smart, responsible.

I ignored the animal part of my brain that wanted his hot cum to brand me deep inside.

His heat left me for mere seconds when he went

to retrieve what we needed from his jeans pocket. He quickly sheathed himself and settled his weight over me once again.

"I need you inside me," I panted, arching my back and rubbing my peaked nipples against his hard chest. "Please, Joseph. I need you."

He bit out a curse, and I felt his hard cock line up with my slick entrance. He pushed in slowly, showing the same care for my wellbeing he'd demonstrated so many times already. He was just as big as I'd imagined, and although he took his time with me, a slight burn accompanied his penetration.

My breath came in short, shallow gasps as I struggled to accommodate him. The way he stretched my body to its limit made me feel almost unbearably full, but I was already addicted to the feel of being completely overwhelmed by him. I welcomed the burn, the edge of discomfort that came along with pleasure.

"Hold on to me," he urged. "I've got you."

Finally, I moved my arms from where they'd been stretched above my head. My fingers curved into his shoulders, clinging to him as he entered me to the hilt. He groaned at the effort of holding himself back, but he remained still inside me for several long seconds. My inner walls contracted around him, struggling to adjust to his size.

He captured my lips in a tender kiss, coaxing my mouth open so his tongue could slide against mine. I sighed and relaxed beneath him, my inner muscles finally easing enough to allow him to move within me. He pulled almost all the way out, his cockhead dragging across my g-spot. Stars burst across my vision as pleasure sizzled through me. When he began to enter me again, I rocked my hips up to meet him, craving more of the blissful stimulation.

He took up a slow, steady pace, stroking into me with care. But I could feel the tension in his lips where they caressed mine, and I knew it was almost painfully difficult for him to restrain himself.

I didn't want him to show any restraint.

I boldly wrapped my legs around him and sank my teeth into his lower lip.

His control snapped. He snarled into my mouth and slammed into me, driving deep and hard. He began to take me without finesse, and I met each of his wild, harsh thrusts. He hit the sensitive spot inside me over and over again, sending me flying impossibly higher.

I cried out, and my core contracted around him as my orgasm rushed through me with blinding force. He kissed me harder, his tongue claiming my mouth in the same way his cock claimed my pussy.

My orgasm triggered his, and he snarled his pleasure as his cock jerked inside me. He'd taken me, marked me as his. The knowledge kept me floating in ecstasy, even as I came down from my high. Little aftershocks of pleasure crackled through my system, and he remained firmly seated inside me, as though he couldn't bear to be parted from me, either.

He grasped my hips and rolled, positioning my body so I was draped over him. I rested my cheek on his sculpted chest, breathing him in as I lingered in bliss. He resumed praising me, murmuring about how beautiful and perfect I was. The residual physical pleasure and the joy elicited by his reverent words cocooned me in a warm glow. I relaxed into him, and his sweet endearments lulled me to sleep.

Chapter Seven
JOSEPH

I should've left half an hour ago, but I lingered in Ashlyn's bedroom while she took a shower. When she'd woken up in my arms this morning, she'd told me I was welcome to stay—her wide eyes had practically begged me to stay—and my half-hearted insistence that I should get going had died on my tongue.

I'd slept at her place again after our explosive sex last night. Part of my mind knew that my long-denied hunger for her had deepened into obsession. I shouldn't be so attached to her this quickly.

And on some level, I knew it wasn't right that I was allowing myself to surrender to her allure. Ashlyn was every bit as sweet and innocent as I'd imagined. Her infatuation with me was obvious—if she weren't infatuated, she would've run scared from my shockingly intense behavior. She was either too young or too inexperienced to understand that chemistry like ours could be dangerous. All-consuming. Reckless.

I didn't have the excuse of youth or inexperience. I'd never felt a connection this strong with any woman, but I should've recognized that things were happening far too fast. I couldn't think through my decisions rationally when I was drunk on her touch and affection. I'd always thrived on control, but with Ashlyn, I had none.

Last night, she'd given me just a taste of what it would be like to have her submit to my darkest desires, and it'd been the hottest experience of my life. She'd surrendered to me, but somehow, I'd lost all control even as I mastered her body. I'd lost myself in *her*, forgetting all the reasons I should proceed with caution.

I'd forgotten about my fucked-up past, my violent family, and my brutal enemies. And in the morning light, it was far too easy to shrug off any thoughts about the darkness I was running from.

Worrying about the mafia was all but impossible while tucked beneath the warmth of Ashlyn's plush, pale pink duvet. Her ivory bedroom walls were sprinkled with small silver stars, and pastel-hued décor enhanced the soft, dreamlike quality of my surroundings.

This could be my world now. I could live a life filled with lazy mornings and Ashlyn's sweet, warm presence at my side.

I'd never again have innocent blood on my hands.

I allowed myself to sink into the fantasy, fully embracing this existence where I belonged in Ashlyn's bed. Where she belonged to me.

Chapter Eight
ASHLYN

I was an idiot. Because I was pretty sure I was falling in love, and that wasn't something I would've thought possible. Certainly not so fast. I'd spent every free moment with Joseph over the last two weeks, and while I still didn't know him well, I couldn't help falling for him. I wasn't accustomed to anyone truly caring about me, and before meeting him, I'd found it difficult to trust people.

With Joseph, I couldn't hold anything back. Not my body and not my heart. We spent most of our time together in bed, but I knew our connection was more than simple physical lust. When he captured me in his crystalline blue stare, there was something worshipful about the light in his eyes. No one had ever looked at me like that. Not a man, not my family.

It was addictive, intoxicating. I craved his nearness, and I hated when I had to leave him to go to class or when he had to work a shift at the bar. After I finished studying in the evenings—something that was becoming increasingly difficult with Joseph taking up my full attention—I went to the bar and tried not to seem like a pathetic stalker. Jayme accompanied me, but it was hard to stay focused on girl talk when Joseph was shooting me heated glances from across the bar.

"Are you even listening to me?" she demanded, clearly irritated with my distraction.

"Sorry, what?" I tore my eyes from Joseph's hypnotic stare and focused on my friend. Her lips were pursed with annoyance.

"I was asking if you want to go to the party at the Fly clubhouse this weekend. You know, if you can manage to pry yourself out of Joseph's arms."

I'd firmly rejected Stu's former invitation, but Jayme had managed to secure one of her own from a blond hottie she'd met a few days after I'd started dating Joseph.

My cheeks heated. "Oh, um, sorry. I should've been paying more attention. But I probably won't go to the party. Sorry," I apologized again.

She waved off my apology with a small smile, my transgression forgiven. "It's okay. Stu's a creepy dick, and I get it if you don't want to risk bumping into him. I'm really happy for you that you're hooking up with the hottest guy in town. Even if I'm super jealous. Although," she purred the word and glanced past me, "this guy might give Joseph a run for his money. And he's totally checking us out. I call dibs, since you're taken."

I grinned at her, happy that she'd found an enticing distraction. "Sure. He's all yours."

"Girl, are you not even going to look? He's freaking gorgeous. Total bad boy, leather jacket vibe. Kind of like Joseph, but…harder. Yummy."

I laughed at her description and turned to look for the mystery man out of idle curiosity, if nothing else.

My laughter caught in my throat when I laid eyes on him.

Hard wasn't a dark enough word to describe him. And he certainly wasn't a *bad boy*. This was a dangerous man. He was older than the students by at least five years, but there was something else about him that further separated him from the boys around him. Maybe it was his leather jacket and motorcycle boots. Or maybe it was his sheer size; he was almost as tall as Joseph, and impossibly broader. His clenched square jaw looked sharp enough to cut, the almost harsh lines of his face roughened further by his dark stubble.

When his black eyes locked on me, I knew none of those physical markers were what set him apart. There was something dark about his soul, something twisted and cold.

One corner of his lips twitched when he caught me looking at him, and I tore my gaze away. My hands were suddenly clammy, my fingers almost trembling.

"I, um, I'm going to the restroom," I announced, needing to escape from his stare. "I'll be right back."

"Sure," Jayme agreed easily. "But if I'm occupied when you get back, don't be offended."

She shot another heated stare in the dark stranger's direction. I didn't understand her attraction. He was obviously bad news. I blinked at her, baffled by her choice in men.

"Be careful," I advised.

She tossed her long blonde hair over her shoulder with a little laugh. "What's the fun in that?"

I shook my head slightly. "He's all yours. I'll hang out at the bar with Joseph to give you some space."

"Thanks, girl."

"Of course. But let me know if you decide to take that guy home. I don't want you to leave with him alone."

"Will do," she promised. "I won't go anywhere alone with a stranger. We can leave with you and Joseph in a few hours." She gave me a sly smile. "We'll make it a double date tonight."

"Sounds good to me. See you soon."

I wound my way through the crowded dance floor and got in line for the bathroom. There were three women in the short corridor ahead of me, but I didn't mind. I hadn't really needed to go, but I'd wanted the excuse to escape from the dark stranger's stare. I wasn't entirely comfortable leaving Jayme at his mercy, but she seemed happy enough with his attention. I wasn't going to cockblock her.

"Are you Ashlyn?" I jolted at the rumbling, masculine voice. It was low and deep, and far too close.

I spun around on a soft gasp, and I found the dangerous stranger in my personal space. The bar was loud enough that I hadn't heard his approach, but now that I was caught in his black stare, I was very aware of his nearness.

I took a step back, and my butt bumped into the wall. His lips curved up at the corners, his harsh eyes flashing with amusement.

"So, are you? You're Ashlyn, right?" he prompted. He didn't step toward me, but he leaned in, his bulk bearing down on me.

My breath stuttered in my throat, and my pulse

hammered in my veins. The dark energy pulsing off him kissed my skin, curling around my body in insidious, velvety tendrils. I shivered, but I wasn't cold.

"What do you want?" I squeaked. I felt thoroughly trapped, even though he wasn't touching me. His intent stare and powerful aura were enough to pin me in place. "How do you know my name?"

"What the fuck are you doing here, Marco? Get away from her."

I sucked in a relieved breath at the sound of Joseph's furious growl. He was coming to my rescue again, and I'd never been more grateful for my knight in shining armor.

Then, something else registered. *Marco.* Joseph knew his name. He knew this intimidating man. I'd known Joseph wasn't from my world; he wasn't a student at Harvard. But I hadn't imagined that the tender man I'd fallen for would associate with someone so overtly dangerous.

Marco's lips curved farther, and he turned his coolly amused gaze on Joseph. "I'm just introducing myself to Ashlyn," he said, nonchalant. "I heard you had a girlfriend. I wanted to meet her."

"Outside. Now," Joseph bit out.

"All right," Marco agreed. I heaved in a deep breath when he finally stepped away from me, freeing me from his influence. He glanced back at me one more time, a sly smirk fixed on his face. "Goodbye, Ashlyn."

Joseph snarled and took a step toward Marco. The frightening man raised his hands in a show of contrition. "Outside," he prompted Joseph.

I didn't want Joseph to leave with him. Marco was a threat, and I didn't want him to hurt the man I loved.

Love. Yes, I was in love with Joseph. The idea of him being hurt made my stomach turn.

I reached out and grabbed his big hand, holding him back. "Don't," I begged. "Stay in here with me."

He stared down at me, his expression drawn with pain that I didn't understand. "I can't," he rasped. He leaned down and brushed a kiss over my lips. "I'm sorry. Stay inside. Don't follow me."

Somehow the words seemed heavier than a simple order not to follow him outside. My heart twisted, my stomach knotting with anxiety. Something was very wrong, and I didn't understand why Joseph would go anywhere with Marco.

Before I could fully process what was happening, Joseph pulled his hand from mine and began making his way through the crowd, following Marco toward the exit. The man I loved disappeared into the night, leaving me behind.

Chapter Nine
JOSEPH

Rage coursed through my veins. Of course Marco had hunted me down. My best friend would never have allowed me to escape from my family. Even though he knew I hated it, I also knew that it'd been selfish for me to leave him behind in that hell.

Secretly, he resented our mafia lifestyle as much as I did, although he'd never admit it aloud. I'd known him long enough to recognize that his cold exterior was a barrier between him and his more volatile emotions. His hard edges concealed a deeply buried pain that he would never express openly, maybe not even to himself.

I couldn't bring myself to hate him, but I could rage at him for ruining my escape.

"Why did you come after me?" I demanded when we stepped outside the ring of illumination provided by the streetlight. "You know I want out. Why would you do this to me?" The last came out more strained than I'd intended.

I didn't want to abandon the simpler life I'd found in Cambridge. I didn't want to abandon Ashlyn and the powerful connection I shared with her. My affection for her bordered on obsession, and there was so much more I wanted to learn about her.

"You know I couldn't let you go," Marco rumbled, crossing his arms over his chest. "There's a war brewing in our family. Tensions are running high. Dominic Russo's son can't just disappear. You know your father will take over as soon as the don passes, which could be any day now. It looks suspicious that you ghosted. Like maybe you didn't leave of your own accord, if you know what I mean. You could've been fucking dead, Joseph." His voice roughened. His hard demeanor threatened to crack, revealing just how much he'd worried about me.

"Then you called me," he continued. "I got the area code off the call and was able to narrow my search. At least I knew you were alive. Do you know what—" He cut himself off, shaking his head sharply. "You have to come back with me. It's going to get bloody if you don't. Do you want your father to be murdered in a power struggle?"

My stomach sank. I hadn't fully thought through the potential ramifications of my disappearance. As much as I hated that life—the violent world I'd been born into—I didn't want to see my father dead.

"No," I said quietly. "Of course not. But I can't go back with you. I can't."

"Yes, you can," he said harshly. "You just don't want to. But you have responsibilities, Joseph. Even if you don't want them, that doesn't mean you don't carry them."

He regarded me for a moment, his head canting to the side as he studied me with his piercing black gaze. "You don't want to leave *her*," he concluded, seeing straight through me. "You know you can't stay near her," he said more gently. "If I can find you, anyone can. It's just a matter of time. Do you really want your father's enemies to get their hands on her?"

My fists curled at my sides, my rage surging once again. "No," I growled, an absolute denial of the idea of Ashlyn in pain, used as a weapon against me.

"Come home with me," he urged. "You don't have a choice. Not if you want to protect her. Not if you want to protect your father. And me," he added, as though that was of little consequence.

I wouldn't risk Marco. The man who was like a

brother to me couldn't be hurt because of my selfish choices. I'd die before I let that happen.

My shoulders slumped as defeat rolled over me. All my foolish dreams of having a normal life with my perfect angel shattered. I was going to have to leave Ashlyn behind.

Chapter Ten
MARCO
One Month Later

My decision was reckless and more than a little selfish. I'd told myself I was doing this for her own good, to protect Ashlyn from potentially being discovered by our enemies.

But really, I was doing this for Joseph. He'd been a shell of himself since returning to New York with me. I knew it had more to do with losing Ashlyn than it did with his hatred of our violent lives. He'd been happy with her, and being torn from her was killing him inside.

I couldn't allow my surrogate brother to suffer like that.

I glanced over at Jayme. The blonde was sleeping soundly on the couch in the apartment she shared with Ashlyn. Seducing her hadn't been difficult. Slipping a roofie into her drink had been laughably easy, and I'd secured an invitation back to her place. I would never violate her, but I'd needed her to let me in. She was a means to an end, and all she'd suffer was a wicked headache in the morning and very little memory of spending any time with me at all.

Ashlyn's disappearance wouldn't be traced back to me. I was anonymous here, unknown by anyone. There was no reason to suspect me.

I fingered the syringe in my pocket and waited in the darkness for her.

Ashlyn was going to come with me, whether she wanted to or not. I'd give her back to Joseph. I'd fix him. They'd both move past my questionable decision to take her against her will. Eventually.

They'd be happy, and maybe I would be too.

Chapter Eleven
ASHLYN

My heart jumped into my throat as soon as I stepped into my darkened apartment. The back of my neck prickled, some primal part of my brain immediately sensing danger. I knew the man was there in the split second before his hand clamped over my mouth. The pressure propelled me backward, and I bumped into the door behind me. His movements weren't violent enough to cause me pain, but they were terrifying enough to make my pulse hammer through my veins. My soft scream was smothered by his big hand.

"Shhh, Ashlyn." He shushed me softly, but steel lurked beneath his horrifyingly gentle tone. "I'm not going to hurt you."

I recognized the voice. I'd heard it once before. The low rumble haunted me in my dreams, leaving me sweating and twisting in my sheets at the memory of the darkness that pulsed from his powerful frame.

Marco. Joseph's frightening acquaintance. Marco, the dangerous man who had appeared one night and stolen the man I loved away from me. He'd made Joseph disappear and abandon me, shattering my heart in the process.

Anger swelled along with fear, and I shoved at Marco's chest. When that accomplished nothing, I curled my fingers into claws, ready to rake my short nails across his face.

He caught my hands easily before I could inflict damage. He released my mouth for a moment while he grasped my wrists. Then, he shifted them into one hand and pinned them over my head. His other hand returned to my mouth to cover my fresh scream.

"I'm not going to hurt you," he said again. "I need you to calm down and listen to me. You're in danger, and I need to get you out of here."

I shook my head as best I could with his firm grip on my face. The only danger was the threat *he* posed.

"You don't understand," he continued. "Joseph didn't tell you about who he really is. Who we are. The kind of men we are. He wanted to shield you from it, but that's over now."

My mind spun, struggling to process what he was saying. What could he possibly mean? Joseph had possessed a sinfully sexy bad boy vibe, but he'd worshipped me. He'd treated me like something precious and called me his *angel*. It was why I'd fallen for him, hard and fast. My first love.

It was why my heart was ravaged and I walked around with a hollow place in my chest, aching deep in my soul for the last month that had passed without him in my life.

"Our enemies will come for you," Marco said. "I won't put you at risk like that. I won't let Joseph go through that. He can't lose you again. Not forever. Not like this. I won't fucking allow it."

Enemies? What the hell was he talking about?

I twisted in his grip, sure that *he* was my enemy. He was pinning me against the wall and smothering my panicked screams. Fear I'd never known rolled over me in a toxic wave, making my head spin and my stomach turn.

Marco stared down at me. The faint streetlight streaming through the windows caught on his features, the shadows enhancing the hard planes of his face and stubble-covered jaw. The light gleamed on his close-cropped dark hair, and the illumination caught in his black eyes. They sparkled with keen intelligence as he considered me.

After a moment, his lips hardened to a thin slash, and he nodded.

"You're not going to come willingly. I can see that. But I planned for this."

He released my wrists, and my hands closed around his forearm, trying to pry his hand away from my mouth so I could let out the scream he was trapping behind my lips.

He swiftly retrieved something from his pocket. Dread weighed like a stone in my stomach when I saw the syringe.

I redoubled my efforts to escape as he removed the cap with his teeth. I tried to kick him, but he was too close for me to get any leverage, his thigh wedged between my legs. My harsh cries caught against his hand, and mindless panic prevented me from fighting effectively. All I could do was try to free my face from his hold, but his strong arm kept me securely pinned despite my frantic efforts.

The needle gleamed in the dim light just before the sting kissed my neck. His movements were careful rather than violent, and there was minimal pain.

Seconds later, the fear that wracked my senses began to fade away. Warmth enfolded me, and I sagged against him. One final whimper of protest slipped through my lips, but my tongue was too heavy to form the pleas for mercy that tickled at the back of my mind.

"Everything will be okay." His promise floated down to me as I sank into darkness. Corded arms closed around me, catching me before I fell.

"You'll be with Joseph again soon," he said, his voice smooth and oddly comforting. "We'll keep you safe."

Safe. With that strange reassurance, I surrendered to the darkness, and the world disappeared.

Chapter Twelve
JOSEPH

"I got you a present," Marco said, a sly smile on his lips that I didn't trust for one second.

I shrugged, unimpressed and uninterested. Nothing interested me these days. Not since I'd lost *her*. I'd tried to run away and find a normal life, and I'd found Ashlyn: my pure, perfect angel.

But Marco had tracked me down and dragged me back into my own personal hell. I didn't want this life of violence and cruelty. All I wanted was to be free of it all. I thought I'd had a chance at that when I met Ashlyn. Now that the dream had crumbled, I was hollow and apathetic.

So I didn't really give a fuck if Marco had gotten me a golden unicorn. Nothing would faze me now.

"Is that why you made me come here?" I

demanded, wondering why he'd invited me to his family's estate on Long Island. I'd been with my father in the city, trying to defend his claim as the head of our family once the current don—Victor Lombardi—passed. And Victor's death of natural causes was imminent.

Unfortunately for my blood relatives, there were other powerful men within our mafia family who wanted to take power. That was why Marco had dragged me home: to protect my dad and his presumptive position. And they'd all been worried that I was dead, so I supposed it was a small mercy for them that I'd finally been found after months of hiding out around the Harvard campus.

Besides, I might not like my life, but I didn't hate my father. I didn't want to see him dead.

And I didn't want to put Marco at risk, either. The man who'd been my lifelong surrogate brother might've been killed if I'd stayed away. He needed me to watch his back, and I'd abandoned him. I knew that must have hurt him, and I still carried guilt over my decision to leave him behind.

So why the fuck had he gotten me a gift?

The sly smile was still fixed on his hard face. "I told you, I got you a present. I had to stash it here. Come inside and see."

I blew out an exasperated sigh, but I stepped

across the threshold and entered the ostentatious mansion. There was enough white marble and gold gilding in the décor to blind a man. The effect was overwhelming, but Marco's father, Leo De Luca, had never been a subtle man, and this was his home. Even if he rarely came here these days. He was too busy defending my father's position from within the city, too. As Dad's best friend, Leo would die to protect him. Just as Marco would do for me.

Marco began walking toward the elegant curved double staircase, and I followed. Curiosity stirred somewhere deep inside me, but it was faint. Nothing really caught my interest these days. Not since I'd lost Ashlyn and my dream of a normal life with her.

When we got to the top of the stairs and turned toward Marco's bedroom, I stopped. Anger—my one familiar emotion—bubbled up.

"Do not tell me you have a girl in there," I warned through gritted teeth. If a three-way was Marco's idea of a *present*, he'd fucked up big time. I wasn't interested in anyone but Ashlyn. The idea of touching another woman made my stomach turn.

His smile sharpened as he turned the knob and pushed the door open. "As a matter of fact, I do."

Just before my rage could rise, all the air was knocked from my chest. I reeled back a step at the horribly entrancing sight before me. She was even more beautiful than I remembered: her alabaster skin practically shined like some otherworldly being, contrasting with the silky dark hair that spilled over the pillows. Her lovely eyes were closed, her long lashes resting on her cheeks.

"Ashlyn." I rasped her name when I finally remembered how to breathe.

I didn't realize I moved, but suddenly, I found myself at her side. I fell to my knees beside the bed where she was laid out on her back. I grasped her hand in mine. It was just as warm and delicate as I recalled in my fantasies.

She didn't respond to my touch in any way; she remained still, her breathing deep and even. Like an enchanted fairytale princess, waiting for her true love's kiss.

The idea made my stomach drop. She wasn't unconscious from some fantastical spell.

Marco had drugged her.

I rounded on him with a snarl, but I didn't move away from her. I couldn't. "What did you do?"

He crossed his arms over his chest and stared down at me. I might have a few inches of height on him, but he was broader. From my kneeling position, he loomed over me. Over Ashlyn.

I shifted my body between them, shielding her

from my best friend. I knew he was a dangerous man, but he'd never done anything to hurt me.

"Why did you do this?" I prompted when he didn't answer my first question. "Why the fuck would you do this to her?"

Didn't he realize what he'd done? I'd left her behind to protect her. If my father's enemies had discovered her, they might have used her to get to me. I was Dad's weak spot, and Ashlyn was mine.

"You missed her," Marco said, as though that was explanation enough for the horrible crime he'd committed. As a career criminal, he wasn't above kidnapping. But abducting Ashlyn was a personal crime against me. He'd put her at risk by bringing her anywhere near me.

I wanted to rage at him. I wanted to attack him, to hurt him in a way I'd never contemplated before.

But I couldn't move away from her. I couldn't let go of her hand. She was so small, vulnerable. I couldn't leave her side, not while she was unconscious and powerless to defend herself.

Not that she could've defended herself against Marco. My brutal friend didn't hurt women, but then again, I'd never have imagined him capable of something like this.

"You abducted her because I *missed her?*" I seethed. "Don't you understand the danger you've put her in? She was safe in Cambridge. She was safe without me." The last declaration left ashes on my tongue.

"No, she wasn't," Marco countered. "I'm not the only one who was looking into your disappearance. I'm not the only one who found your hiding place at Harvard."

My pulse pounded through my veins. Guilt and selfish hope tormented me. If Ashlyn had been discovered by my father's enemies, then Marco hadn't had a choice. He'd taken her to protect her.

But that meant I was ultimately responsible for ripping her from her pretty, perfect life. I'd never wanted that for her. All I'd wanted was to cherish her and make her blissfully happy.

That wasn't reality, though. My reality was bloody and brutal, and I'd brought her into this tainted world.

"We didn't have a choice," Marco continued. I barely noticed the *we*. Marco and I were a team, and while he'd made this decision on his own, I was now complicit in it.

Because I wasn't going to let her go. Not again. I couldn't now that I was near her.

The fact that she might be in danger if I wasn't here to protect her was an excuse to keep her. Some part of my mind knew that. If I were truly a good man, I'd tell her to go to the police for protection.

But at heart, I was a selfish, hungry bastard. I wanted her, and while I'd been noble enough to leave her once, I couldn't do it again. I wouldn't.

I turned back to look at her, to drink in the sight of her. I could still feel Marco's presence at my back, but I didn't care. He knew all my secrets, and his watchful eyes on us barely registered.

Unable to resist her allure, I reached out and traced the line of her cheekbone with my thumb, trailing my fingertips along her jaw. I wanted to memorize every contour of her face, her body. Even my bittersweet, obsessive memories couldn't compare to having her here with me.

A little furrow appeared between her brows, and she let out a low groan. Despite the sound of discomfort, she leaned her cheek into my hand.

"Joseph?" she asked groggily, somewhere between sleep and wakefulness.

The sound of my name on her tongue went straight to my cock, and I immediately stiffened for her. Yearning and lust raged through my system, and my hand tightened around hers.

From that moment, I knew I wouldn't be capable of ever letting her go again.

Chapter Thirteen
ASHLYN

"It's me. I'm right here. I've got you, angel."

I recognized Joseph's deep voice, the smooth tone he used when he told me how beautiful I was.

Despite my headache, I sighed and leaned into his touch. I kept my eyes closed as I reveled in the feel of his hand against my cheek, touching me with the careful reverence he'd always reserved for me. He was so big and strong, but he held me like something precious and fragile. His gentle hold was often at odds with the fierce way he kissed me; he worshipped me and devoured me at the same time. I found the combination addictive. I found *him* addictive.

I longed to look into his eyes again. My lashes fluttered against the sudden wash of light, and I squinted as my pupils adjusted. When the world came into focus, I found myself captured in his beautiful, aquamarine gaze. Twin blue flames flickered in his eyes as he studied me with the familiar hunger that made my blood race.

His lashes were just as long and thick as I remembered, his mouth just as full and sensual. More dark stubble covered his strong, square jaw than usual, as though he hadn't shaved in several days. His glossy black curls fell around his face, his hair a bit unrulier than the last time I'd seen him. Even slightly unkempt, he was the most breathtaking thing I'd ever seen.

"Joseph," I rasped, his name catching in my parched throat.

His brows drew together. "She needs water." He wasn't addressing me, but sleep still fogged my mind too thickly for me to contemplate it.

"On the nightstand." I recognized that voice, too. It was the one that haunted my dreams, the voice that had whispered through the darkness as the needle pricked my neck...

Marco.

I sat up with a gasp as the memory of his attack flooded my mind. The sharp intake of air tormented my dry throat, and I coughed. My head throbbed and spun at my sudden movements. I swayed, and

Joseph's strong arm closed around my back before I could fall.

"It's okay," he promised. "You're safe. Drink."

A cool glass touched my lips, and I gulped down the water without thinking of protesting. I'd never been able to deny Joseph when he issued those low, self-assured commands.

When I'd drained half the glass, he took it away and set it aside. The mattress dipped beside me as he sat on the bed, cuddling me close. I leaned into him, breathing him in as he pressed a tender kiss against my pounding head.

"Just breathe," he cajoled. "You're okay."

"She'll be fine. She just needs to stay hydrated."

I stiffened at the sound of Marco's voice. He was talking about me as though I wasn't here, and I bristled. He'd shown no consideration for my wishes or wellbeing when he'd freaking drugged and kidnapped me.

I looked past Joseph to glare at Marco. His black eyes stared right back at me, implacable. He obviously didn't feel a shred of remorse for what he'd done to me. His blank expression betrayed no emotion at all.

I shrank closer to Joseph. I looked back at him, unable to maintain eye contact with the dangerous man who loomed over us, his corded arms crossed over his massive chest. Marco oozed danger, a darkness that emanated from his soul. I'd felt it the first time I'd met him, and I definitely felt it now. He'd attacked me, abducted me. The memory of those strong arms pinning me against the wall and smothering my panicked screams made me shudder. Joseph's hand stroked up and down my back, soothing me.

"I've got you," he promised again.

I stared up into his beautiful eyes, imploring. "What's happening? Why is *he* here?"

I recalled Marco telling me that he was taking me to Joseph. I wasn't frightened of the man I loved, but I didn't understand why he wasn't shielding me from his terrifying friend. I didn't understand why he wasn't coming to my rescue and taking me back to my apartment at Harvard.

"He's here to protect you, just like I am."

Joseph's words didn't make any sense.

"He *kidnapped* me." There was no way Marco was trying to protect me. He was my enemy, a threat. He certainly wasn't a white knight, not like Joseph. Joseph had always defended me. He'd saved me from Stu when the creep had tried to touch me without my permission. He wouldn't allow his scary friend to get away with abducting me.

"To keep you safe," Joseph countered calmly, but

his eyes tightened with anxiety. "I'm sorry, Ashlyn. This is my fault." His arm firmed around me. "But I can't leave you alone and at risk. I tried, and it didn't work."

My mind churned, struggling to piece together what he was saying. My heart had shattered the night he'd walked out of my life. Now, he was trying to tell me why, but I couldn't wrap my head around it.

"What are you saying? Why did you leave me?" My voice was small, the familiar pain of his loss stabbing through my chest. He might be holding me, but that didn't fully erase the torment he'd put me through when he'd left.

"I'm not...good for you." He stumbled over the admission. "I don't deserve you. I knew it from the beginning, so I tried to keep my distance. I saw you at the bar for weeks, but I didn't let myself near you. Then, that asshole Stu touched you, and I couldn't hold back. It was selfish of me."

I remembered that night vividly. From the moment he'd rescued me, we'd been inseparable. Our relationship had been short, but I'd never felt so connected to any man. I'd fallen for Joseph, hard and fast.

But he left me. I still didn't understand why.

"What do you mean?" I pressed. "Why do you think you don't deserve me? All you ever did was protect me and make me happy. I..." I stopped myself from confessing my feelings for him. We'd never gotten to the point of exchanging the words *I love you*. With the uncertainty that plagued me, I knew now wasn't the time.

His lips pressed to a thin line, and his eyes dropped so he was no longer looking at me. He was shutting down, shutting me out.

"Tell me what's going on," I demanded, frustrated. I was rarely so assertive with Joseph—he usually took the lead—but when he was trying to isolate himself from me, I couldn't allow it. Especially when I needed to know what the hell was happening. He wasn't really answering any of my questions.

"I don't understand why you're being such an angsty teenager, Joseph," Marco said, his voice clipped with annoyance that mirrored my own. "If you won't tell her, I will."

Marco paused, giving him a moment to speak. Joseph swallowed hard and kept his gaze averted from mine. He still didn't put an inch of space between us, as though he couldn't stop touching me. I didn't want him to. After a month of emptiness without him, I craved his nearness.

But that didn't mean I didn't want answers.

"Fine," Marco sighed. His black eyes fixed on me, and I couldn't look away. His expression was cool, detached. But there was something sharper in his eyes, a deeper emotion that I didn't understand.

"We're mafia, Ashlyn. Joseph and I are part of the Lombardi crime family. We were born into it. This is who we are."

I shook my head, an absolute refusal to believe it. Joseph might have a bad boy sense of style and an intimidating physique, but he'd always treated me with tenderness. He was kind, good down to his core. He couldn't be a criminal.

"You're lying."

"I'm not. Tell her, Joseph."

His aquamarine gaze lifted to mine, his eyes tight with anguish.

"Tell me he's lying," I begged, but I could read the truth in the taut lines of his face.

"It's true." His admission was little more than a whisper.

I pulled away from him, my stomach turning. Everything we'd shared—trust, love—began to crumble in my chest. He'd never told me much about himself; we'd always talked about *me*. Well, we'd talked when we weren't tangled in the sheets, communicating our feelings with our bodies.

I put more distance between us, realizing I didn't know the man beside me at all.

He didn't reach for me. He dropped his arms at

his sides, his hands clenching to fists. He wasn't looking at me anymore.

"Jesus, Joseph, what happened to your balls?" Marco asked, exasperated. "This whole *Romeo and Juliet*, star-crossed-lovers thing is stupid. Get over yourself and explain what's happening. You owe her that much."

Joseph glowered at him. "You're the one who kidnapped her. *You* explain."

"You're acting like a child," Marco drawled. "But fine. If I have to be the bad guy, I'll be the bad guy. You can keep pretending to be noble, but that's bullshit, and you know it. You want to keep her. Admit it."

"*Keep me?*" I demanded. "I'm a human being. Stop talking about me like I'm an object."

Marco fixed me in his implacable stare again, and I froze. "I can see that you're going to be just as dramatic about this as Joseph. Calm down and listen."

It was a clear order, and there was a subtle threat behind it. An unspoken *or else*.

I didn't want to find out what the *or else* was. I didn't think Joseph would let him hurt me, but then again, it seemed I didn't know Joseph at all.

"I took you because you're in danger, Ashlyn," Marco explained away his crime as though he'd done me a favor. "Joseph was hiding out in Cambridge for a few months. I found him, though. And he was lucky I did. His father has enemies, and they were looking for him, too. Even after I dragged him back home, they kept digging. They found out he'd been dating you while he was living there. If I hadn't taken you away, they might have gotten to you first and used you as leverage against us."

"This is insane." I shook my head, struggling with everything he was telling me. Yesterday, I'd been a normal college student, pining for my first love. Now, I was involved with the mafia? It was crazy. Absolutely nuts.

"This is reality," Marco said harshly. "You led a charmed life at Harvard, with your fancy apartment and your fancy education. But you need to start living in the real world, little girl."

I skipped past indignation at being called *little girl*. I went straight to royally pissed off. The way he described my life made me sound like a cosseted child. He didn't know me at all.

"Take me back," I seethed. "If you are who you say you are, I don't want to be anywhere near you. Take me back to school."

"No." It was an unequivocal refusal. "If I take you back, you could get hurt. I won't do that to Joseph."

"You won't do that to *Joseph*? What about what you're doing to *me*?" I folded my arms over my chest, imitating his hard stance. "Take me back." I enunciated each word, righteous anger giving me the courage to stand up to him.

Suddenly, he moved toward me. He'd been intimidating while standing still as a granite statue. He loomed impossibly larger as he closed the distance between us, prowling with lethal grace. My breath caught in my throat, and when he got into my personal space, I forgot how to breathe.

He leaned over me, bringing his arms up around me and resting his palms on the headboard. His huge body caged me in, his powerful aura pinning me in place. His face was inches from mine, and his black eyes swallowed me up.

"Do you want to be murdered? Or maybe they'll just rape you. Or maybe they'll pass you around until they get bored, and then they'll kill you. Is that what you want?"

My mouth went dry, and my hands began to tremble as the awful words rumbled from his chest.

"Back off, Marco," Joseph growled. "You're scaring her."

Marco didn't move away from me. "She should be scared. She needs to know what will happen to her if she tries to leave." He was speaking to Joseph about me again, but I couldn't muster up any anger over it this time. I was too frightened to be angry.

"You're not going anywhere. Certainly not back to Harvard. You're not going to leave this house until we say you can. Do you understand?"

I shook my head slightly, a weak denial of the horror I faced.

"Back. Off." Joseph tried to come to my defense again, but Marco didn't listen.

"You're going to tell your family, friends, and professors that you're taking some time off from school," he informed me, his hard tone brooking no discussion over the matter. "You're going to stay here with us. Do you understand?" he asked again, demanding only one answer.

I swallowed and nodded, knowing he wouldn't accept anything else. He'd remain here, trapping me, until I agreed. Or maybe he'd do worse than getting in my personal space. Every word he spoke dripped dark authority, and I was too intimidated to continue defying him.

"Good girl." He finally withdrew, and I heaved in a gasping breath.

My heart hammered in my chest as though I'd run a mile, and my hands shook. Fear was venom in my veins, coursing through my body with insidious intent. Tears stung at the corners of my eyes, and I tried to take deep breaths to stave them off. My chest seized. Drawing in air became difficult as my breaths came faster and faster. I was close to hyperventilating, panic setting in as Marco's horrific words echoed in my mind.

Maybe they'll pass you around until they get bored, and then they'll kill you.

He had told me this was my new reality: remain his captive or face rape and death at the hands of their enemies.

I couldn't process it. I was just a privileged, damaged girl from Georgia who had worked hard to earn her place at a prestigious university. My whole life had been about getting a good education and making my father proud. Then, Joseph came into my life, and my world shifted to revolve around *him*. I'd yearned to have him back, but now that I was with him again, everything was horribly wrong.

Mafia. Joseph is a mobster.

The concept could barely penetrate my consciousness. Not only was it abhorrent, but I'd been convinced that the man I loved was gentle and good, despite his fierce protective streak.

I blinked hard to clear the tears from my vision, searching for Joseph's gaze. He was watching me, his jaw tight and his fists still clenched at his sides.

"I'm so sorry, angel," he rasped.

I latched onto his contrition. "You don't have to do this," I pleaded. "You don't want to hurt me. I know you don't. Just take me back to school. I won't tell anyone about this. I swear. Just let me go."

His chin lifted, and his eyes blazed with a possessive light I'd seen before. In the past, it had made my toes curl. Now, the depth of his obsession made my stomach drop.

"I can't do that. I won't."

"Finally, the truth," Marco said, smugly satisfied.

"You can't keep me here!" I railed. "I don't want to be part of this. Just let me go back to my life."

"Marco already explained that we can't do that," Joseph said, his resolve hardening to match his friend's. "You're staying right here. With me."

He reached for me, but I shoved at his chest. "I don't want to be with you!" I shouted, my tears falling faster as my heart broke all over again. I could taste the lie on my tongue, but my head knew better than my heart. It didn't matter that my body still longed for his touch. Joseph was toxic, every bit as dangerous as Marco. I just hadn't been able to see it before.

His expression darkened, his jaw ticking. He stopped hunching in shame, sitting up to his full, impressive height. This was the powerful man who'd made my mouth water and my panties damp. Even now, my sex heated in response to the sudden shift in his demeanor.

My helpless response caused rage to surge alongside my panic. Before I knew what I was doing, my hand cracked across his face.

I instantly regretted it. Not only did my palm smart where it had connected with his sharp cheekbone, but his expression darkened further.

My animal brain kicked in my flight response, and I tried to scoot away from him.

I didn't make it to my feet before he was on me. He easily caught my wrists as his body settled over mine. His weight pinned me down, his vastly superior strength keeping my hands trapped above my head.

My rage and fear left me on a defiant shriek, and I writhed beneath him. I felt his cock stiffen against my thigh, and my sex grew slick for him: an ingrained response.

I should've been terrified that he might violate me, but that thought never registered. Deep down, I knew Joseph would never hurt me. He wasn't capable of it, no matter what kind of violent lifestyle he led. Even now, he held me carefully, restraining me firmly without causing me pain.

But I couldn't stop fighting. He'd denied my instinct for flight, and fight was all I had left.

I turned my head and sank my teeth into his forearm. He cursed and jerked his arm away, but he didn't back off. Keeping his hold on my wrists, his free hand settled over the front of my throat, his long fingers wrapping around my neck. He didn't apply any pressure, but the act of dominance shocked me into silence. My screams stopped abruptly, and I went still beneath him.

He stared down at me, a dark satisfaction in his eyes that I'd seen before but never fully understood. He liked overpowering me. I'd thought it was a kinky game when we'd engaged in this kind of play.

But Joseph wasn't *playing*. He was demonstrating his absolute power over me, showing me that there was no point in fighting him. He would always win, and he would enjoy subjugating me.

My lower lip quivered, and Joseph leaned in to press a gentle kiss against it.

"Don't cry, angel," he cooed. "I'll keep you safe."

His calloused fingertips stroked the column of my neck, lighting up my sensitive nerve endings. I bit back a moan as memories of ecstasy at his touch assailed me. My body was conditioned to respond to him. Or maybe I'd been this powerless against him from the very beginning.

I certainly felt powerless now: conquered and completely overwhelmed.

He brushed his soft lips over my cheeks, kissing away my tears.

His hand was still wrapped around my throat. He

was still pinning my wrists above my head. And his cock was still hard against my hip.

"Are you finished with your little tantrum, then?" Marco's drawl penetrated the intense connection between Joseph and me. I was almost grateful for his mocking words. At least they freed me from the power Joseph held over me.

Heat crept up my neck, and I turned my face away from Joseph's kisses. Embarrassment burned my cheeks. Marco was watching us, observing us. His keen black eyes studied me, and I got the sense that he could read every nuance of my emotions.

"Please," I begged Joseph. "Get off me." I couldn't bear his touch for one more second, especially not with Marco watching.

He didn't comply right away.

"Are you going to continue acting like a brat?" Marco asked me. "If you're ready to behave, Joseph can let you up."

My cheeks flamed hotter. I didn't want to agree to *behave*. It was tantamount to admitting that I'd been acting like a naughty child. I didn't understand how Joseph could allow Marco to talk to me this way.

But Joseph wasn't letting me up. He was waiting for my response. Again, I knew there was only one answer they would accept.

"Okay," I managed on a whisper. "I'll..." I couldn't

bring myself to say the words *I'll behave.* "I won't try to fight you."

Marco's hard lips twitched with amusement, stoking my embarrassment into indignation.

Still, when Joseph finally released me, I didn't try to run. There was no point. Marco stood between me and the door, and Joseph had just proven how easily he could catch me and trap me.

With as much dignity as I could muster, I sat upright and smoothed my hands over my hair, straightening the places where it'd become mussed during my struggles. When I felt somewhat more collected, I took a breath and faced Marco head-on, spearing him with a defiant glare.

A wide, wicked grin spread out on his face, the first true smile I'd ever seen him wear.

It was even more intimidating than his cold stare, and I wouldn't have thought that possible.

Chapter Fourteen
ASHLYN

"Here." Marco handed me a notebook and a pen.

"What's this for?" I still sat on the bed, but I'd scooted as far away from Joseph as I could manage. Marco remained standing, and that unnerved me even more than Joseph's nearness.

"You're going to write some emails," Marco told me.

I blinked at him, nonplussed. "Emails. With a pen and paper."

He nodded. "You write them, I'll type and send them. If you think we're letting you anywhere near a laptop, you're mistaken."

"What am I supposed to write?" I was pretty sure *Help! I've been kidnapped by mobsters!* wasn't going to be an acceptable message. Just the fact that this was my new reality had barely begun to sink in. If it weren't for Marco's intimidating presence, I might have giggled at the absurdity of it all.

But there was nothing funny about Marco's dark stare.

"I want three emails," he said, ticking each off his fingers as he spoke. "One to your family, one to your roommate, and one for your professors. You'll explain that you're going through a hard time—I'm sure they've all seen what a mess you've been after losing Joseph—and you'll say—"

"Excuse me?" I cut him off. "A *mess?*"

He raised one dark brow. "Yes. A mess. I had people watching you. Do you want to see the before and after photos? I have some from when you were with Joseph, and several after that. If it makes you feel better, he doesn't usually look this shitty, either. He's actually pretty vain, to be honest."

"Don't listen to him," Joseph said, his voice all warmth and sincerity. "You're beautiful, angel."

"I didn't say she wasn't beautiful. I just said she was a mess after you left." Marco's words were a little defensive, but he didn't sound at all contrite. If anything, he seemed annoyed with the exchange, as though it was of no consequence.

"So, before you interrupted me," he speared me with a warning look, "I was telling you what you'll write in your emails. You need to sound genuine, so that's why you have to write them instead of me making shit up for you. What you say is up to you, but keep it vague. Assure everyone that you're all right."

"And where am I supposed to say I'm staying while I'm on this little sabbatical?" Some of my fire was returning now that Joseph wasn't holding me down, and I made my question as cutting as I dared.

Marco shrugged. "I'm sure your family can afford for you to go on a spa getaway or to some fancy chalet. I honestly don't care what you come up with. Just make it sound real."

"You don't know anything about my family," I declared, my temper flaring.

"So you're saying they can't afford it?"

"That's not the point." My dad had never denied me anything I wanted, but that didn't mean I hadn't worked hard to earn my place at Harvard. Not only had I excelled in academics, but I'd put in countless hours with the swim team during high school, and I'd volunteered as a tutor twice a week.

Marco made it sound as though I was some entitled snob who thought money could buy me anything.

"The point is that you convince them," he said sternly. "Say whatever you need to say, but know that

I'm going to read through them all very carefully to make sure you're not dropping any hints about where you really are."

"I don't even know where I really am." I threw up my hands, exasperated.

"You're at my family's estate. You don't need to know exactly where. All you need to know is that this is where you'll be staying indefinitely. Now, write." He pointed at the notepad, the simple gesture sharp with authority.

"And what about tomorrow? What about next week? What do I say when they ask when I'm coming back?"

"You'll explain that you need time to yourself. Will your parents expect to hear from you every day?"

I cut my eyes away to hide the pain he'd just uncovered, but my hesitation gave him the answer he needed.

"I'll take that as a *no*," he said, cruelly clinical about my estrangement from my family. "I'll monitor their responses and let you know when you need to send another email."

I lifted my chin, hurt making me defiant. "And how do you plan to access my email account?"

He fixed me with a level look. "You're going to give me your username and password."

I scoffed. "Not happening." The fact that I was missing was all that gave me hope. Someone would wonder where I was soon. They'd look for me. The police would get involved. They'd find me and keep me safe from my captors and their enemies.

Marco cocked his head at me, considering. After a moment, he gave a short nod in Joseph's direction. "You deal with her. I'm over this bratty bullshit. Let me know when it's handled."

I gaped at his back as he walked out of the room and shut the door behind him.

Deal with me? Bratty bullshit?

The man was as infuriating as he was intimidating.

I rounded on Joseph, emboldened now that Marco was gone. "How can you let him talk to me like that?" I demanded. "Actually, he's not even doing me the courtesy of talking to me. He's talking to you *about* me while I'm right freaking here. You're just going to let him treat me this way? You're just going to let him kidnap me and talk down to me like I'm nothing?"

Joseph's brows drew together. "He's not treating you like you're nothing. That's just how Marco is. And he only took you to keep you safe. We've explained this."

I rolled my eyes. "Yes, how magnanimous of you.

Instead of warning me and allowing me to go to the police for protection, you've chosen to abduct me and hold me against my will."

"I don't trust the police to keep you safe," he said, suddenly fierce. "I don't trust anyone else to keep you safe. I left you because I thought it was the only way to protect you. If I'd known you were at risk, I never would have let you leave my sight."

I glowered at him. "Marco was right about one thing. You need to stop pretending to be noble. You're not my white knight. You're a criminal, Joseph. You lied to me." The last came out on a strained whisper as my heart twisted at the words.

Shame colored his cheeks. "I didn't lie. I just didn't tell you everything."

"You didn't tell me *anything*," I accused. "Every time I asked about your family or where you were from, you shut me out or changed the subject. I trusted you. I told you everything you ever asked about my life. But I don't know you at all."

"I'm sorry. I didn't want you to know. I was trying to get away from my life. That's why I was in Cambridge. I wanted to hide out and start over. I wanted to start over with you, Ashlyn. Even though I knew I didn't deserve that kind of second chance."

"What did you do in your life that was so terrible?" I flung at him, even though I feared the answer.

His jaw firmed, and he cut his gaze away. "Plenty. And now I've ruined your life. That's the worst crime I could ever commit. All I wanted was for you to be safe and happy." His eyes snapped back up to mine, hard with determination. "I know I've made it impossible for you to be happy, but I'll keep you safe, no matter what. Now, you're going to write these emails and give me your login information."

I pursed my lips. "You're starting to sound like Marco."

"Marco is being hard on you because he wants to keep you safe, too. We just want to protect you."

"He doesn't even know me. Why would he care about me at all?"

His pale eyes glittered, and I became mesmerized by their crystalline shine. "He cares about you because I care about you."

My heart ached. Were the words as heavy with meaning as I imagined?

I love you. The unspoken sentiment was still locked in my chest. Did he feel the same way?

Even after everything I'd learned about him in the last hour, I still felt that soul-deep pull toward him.

"I know you can't forgive me, but at least let me keep you safe. Write the messages. Marco will make sure they get to the right people. It'll buy us time to figure out what to do next."

"I..." I swallowed back my refusal. His earnest expression tugged at my heartstrings. He really did want to protect me, like he'd done from the very beginning. Marco had made it clear that he wasn't going to let me go. If I didn't really have the option to go to the police for protection, then I had to rely on Joseph.

Marco's description of what their enemies would do to me had shaken me to my core.

"Hey," Joseph said gently, calling my attention away from the horrific images that were filling my mind.

His hand covered mine, his thumb stroking my palm. His sincere aqua gaze pierced my soul. "I'd die before I'd let anyone hurt you," he swore.

I found myself nodding. He spoke the absolute truth, and I couldn't hate him when he made such a stark declaration.

"Okay," I whispered. "I'll write the emails."

He lifted my hand to his lips and brushed a kiss over my knuckles. "Thank you."

His touch was electric, and even the chaste gesture made my body light up with awareness. Our eyes caught, and he didn't let go of my hand. He kept his gentle grip on me as he leaned in, closing the distance I'd put between us. My pulse ticked up, and my lips tingled in anticipation of his fierce kiss. Just like it had always been with him, I was completely in his thrall. He didn't have to pin me down to keep me under his power. I was helpless to fight this irresistible connection between us.

He was close enough that his warm breath teased over my lips. They parted, ready for his tongue to sweep into my mouth, claiming me with deep, domineering strokes. His eyes roved over my face, studying me as though he was trying to memorize my every feature. His obsession was intoxicating, his reverence enthralling.

"Ashlyn." He almost groaned my name, his husky tone heavy with longing and a hint of wonder. "I thought I'd never see you again," he murmured.

He reached up and traced the line of my lower lip with his thumb, the touch feather-light and worshipful.

I love you. I bit the words back just before they could roll off my tongue. As much as I ached for his kiss, a new darkness tainted our connection.

Joseph had deceived me. I couldn't trust him.

I remembered how he'd pinned me down and kissed the tears on my cheeks. Mere minutes had passed since then, and the memory of his arousal at my subjugation was still clear in my mind.

Just as he leaned in to capture my lips, I managed to turn my face away.

"Don't," I begged softly. I couldn't bear it if he kissed me. My heart was already in pieces, and I couldn't take any more. The man I loved had ripped my life away from me. He'd put me in danger, and he'd taken away my choices. I'd been convinced that he was good, but now, I didn't know him at all.

I heard him take a shuddering breath. He didn't withdraw immediately. I wondered if he was struggling to hold back the darker part of himself that wanted to pin me down and devour me, to draw out my lust for him until I forgot why I should push him away.

A twisted part of me longed for him to do it, because that would absolve me of any foolishness for falling back into his arms.

Resolutely, I kept my gaze averted from his, denying our connection. Denying *him*.

A low sound of displeasure left his chest, but he finally withdrew. I allowed myself to breathe again, willing my racing pulse to slow to a normal rhythm.

He didn't say anything to me, but I could feel his eyes on me. I didn't look at him. Instead, I picked up the notepad and pen and began writing with shaky hands. I made my excuses to my professors first, then Jayme. She was fully aware of how heartbroken I'd been since Joseph left, so I knew she wouldn't doubt my supposed decision to take time off from school.

I wrote to my father last. There was no point sending an email to my mother. The most I ever got from her were text messages a few times a year, usually filled with falsely cheery emojis. She liked to pretend we had a gal-pal friendship, but that was a fake act to make her feel better. It only left me feeling empty.

Tears began to blur my vision as I made my excuses to my father. All I'd ever wanted was for him to be proud of me, to prove I was worthy of attention and affection. This email would destroy all my hard work. He'd never understand or forgive a rash decision to take time off from college because of heartache over a guy. I could easily imagine the look of disappointment on his face, his bushy gray mustache turning down in a sad frown. It was the same look he'd given me every time I'd failed to be anything less than perfect in my life. I'd told myself he was just pushing me to be a high achiever, but that didn't take the hurt away.

By the time I'd scrawled "Love, Ashlyn," my tears dripped down my face and splattered on the ruled notebook paper. The black ink smudged where they fell, but the message was still legible.

Joseph tugged the notepad out of my hands before I could completely ruin the words I'd written.

"What's your username?" he prompted gently.

"*Abmeyers*. My first initials and last name."

"What's your middle name?"

He'd never asked me before. There was so much we'd never learned about one another, but he was far more of a mystery than I was.

"Bailey," I said dully. I felt hollowed-out, exhausted.

"That's a beautiful name."

I nodded at the compliment, not really listening. Mentally, I was checking out. Everything that'd happened since I'd woken up to find Joseph and Marco looming over me was too much for me to fully process. And the knowledge that my father was going to be disappointed in me rested heavy on my heart.

"And your password?"

"The word Number, capitalized-one-unicorn-exclamation point." I was too wrung out to even feel embarrassed by admitting my childish password.

He paused, but I barely noticed. "Thank you."

I nodded again in rote acknowledgment. My whole situation was becoming surreal, and I sank into the sense of detachment from my emotions. It was so much easier than facing the pain of Joseph's betrayal.

He reached out to brush the wetness from my cheeks, but I flinched away. I laid down and rolled onto my side, drawing my knees up to my chest in a protective position. I didn't want to look at him. I couldn't bear to fall into his gorgeous eyes and fall prey to his allure again. My heart couldn't take it.

He retrieved a blanket from the foot of the bed and tucked it around me.

I closed my eyes, trying to shut him out. "Leave me alone," I mumbled into the pillow.

He said nothing for a long moment, but I could feel him considering me. Finally, I heard his heavy boots stomping across the room, and the door thumped closed behind him.

I heaved in a breath, and a sob ripped from my chest when I exhaled. I pulled the blanket over my head and cried myself to sleep.

Chapter Fifteen
JOSEPH

I stormed down the hall, searching for Marco. Since Ashlyn was stashed in his bedroom, I assumed he'd be in his other favorite room in the house: the kitchen.

Her muffled sobs followed me as I raced down the stairs, taking them two at a time in my haste to escape the sound of her pain. I couldn't do anything to make it go away. She'd made it clear that my presence only made it worse for her.

Impotent fury pounded through my veins, and I knew there was one way I could channel it. I could beat the shit out of Marco.

He was the one who'd kidnapped her. He was the one who'd frightened her.

Ashlyn was gentle, fragile. She needed to be handled with care, shielded and protected. And he'd been just as brutally blunt with her as he was with everyone else.

When I raged into the kitchen, Marco turned away from the sandwich he'd been making. He didn't appear remotely surprised when I swung at him, and he didn't flinch away. My fist connected squarely with his jaw. Familiar pain cut into my knuckles, but it was nothing. I was used to it.

What I wasn't used to was punching my best friend. We'd fought in the past—like brothers do—but I'd never felt this searing anger toward him before.

I pulled my next punch, but my other hand fisted in his shirt. I yanked him toward me so I could snarl in his face.

His black eyes stared at me, implacable as ever.

"Do you feel better now?" he asked coolly, not making a move to retaliate or defend himself. "Does punching me make you feel like the good guy here?"

"Fuck you," I growled. I wasn't used to cussing at him, either. Not in anger.

He shrugged. "I'll give you one more shot, if it'll help you calm down and be reasonable. You're acting like a pissy teenager. I need you to snap out of that shit and face this like a man."

I dropped my fist and released him, shoving him away with another curse. It didn't feel right to hit him, especially when he wasn't fighting back.

"You scared her," I accused, my voice still rough with residual ire. "You made her cry."

"She needed to know the reality of the situation. Would you prefer she hate you for kidnapping her? She has to understand the danger she faces if she's not with us."

"I'm not the one who kidnapped her," I flung back. "You made that decision on your own."

His dark brows rose to his close-cropped black hair. "And if I'd told you that your father's enemies were watching her? What would you have done?"

I ran a hand through my hair. "I would have gone back to her," I hedged, unwilling to admit that I would've done anything to keep her safe, including taking her away from Harvard.

Marco crossed his arms over his chest. "You would've done the same thing I did. I made the choice so you didn't have to. Now, you don't have to feel guilty about it. She'll come around and forgive you. I'm the bad guy here, remember?" His lips twisted slightly on the last part, but the expression was gone so quickly, I might have imagined it.

I finally shook my head, my rage draining out of me. "You did what you had to do. You did what I would've done, even if I don't like it. I didn't know you had people watching her. If you hadn't done that... If you hadn't known and gotten to her in time..." I couldn't bring myself to vocalize the horrors she might have endured. Because of me.

I scrubbed a hand over my face. "I never should've touched her. I should've stayed away."

"Yes, you probably should have. But you shouldn't have run away from New York in the first place. That was a shitty thing to do, Joseph."

"I know." I was surprised he hadn't punched me for that transgression. I'd left without a word and covered my tracks. I could've been dead, for all Marco knew. I'd left my closest friend in the world hanging on to hope that I'd somehow survived the war brewing within our family. When all along, I'd been playing the part of humble bartender while I pretended Ashlyn's safe, simple life could be mine, too.

I'd been a complete fucking idiot, deluding myself into thinking that was a remote possibility. I'd never be free from my violent world.

"I'll never deserve her," I said, not realizing I spoke the words aloud.

"Stop that shit right now," Marco commanded. "I'm done with this lovesick drama. You're not living in a fucking fairytale, Joseph. There are no white knights and evil villains. You don't have to be one or the other. This is the real world. It's ugly and complicated, and it's time you faced that reality and stopped trying to run away or deny it. You're a hard man in a hard world. Start acting like it."

"You mean like you act?" I shot back. "Drugging innocent women and stealing them in the night before scaring them into cooperating? I don't want to be that kind of man, Marco. You know me better than that."

He barely flinched as I flung the accusations at him, but that was enough to let me know I'd cut him deeply.

"And I guess you know me so well, then, if that's what you think of me."

I held my glare for a few seconds, but I dropped my aggression on a sigh. "Sorry, Marco. That was shitty of me. I know you're not a bad person. I know you did what you had to do to keep Ashlyn safe. I just can't stand seeing her cry. It's fucking me up. She hates me now. She wouldn't even look at me."

He clapped me on the shoulder, a comforting gesture. My cruelty was easily forgiven.

"She doesn't hate you. She's just upset. I saw the way she looked at you. Believe me, she's not capable of hating you. Give her some time, and she'll come around. She just needs some space to process everything and accept the situation. She must be a smart girl; she goes to Harvard. It won't take her long to figure out that we really are trying to protect her, not hurt her."

All I could do was hope he was right about that. The thought of Ashlyn flinching away from my touch was enough to sour my stomach. It'd felt fundamentally wrong for her to shy away from my hand, to be frightened of me. I'd do everything in my power to fix this. But for now, Marco was right. She needed space and a little time to rest and process her situation.

"I should go see my father," I said. "He needs to know that Ashlyn is here." I didn't want to hide anything from Dad. Even though I'd tried to run away, he still loved me. He'd help me protect Ashlyn if I told him how important she was to me.

"Yes, you should," Marco agreed. "And it'll give Ashlyn some breathing room if you're gone. Don't worry," he added before I could voice my concerns. "I won't scare her again. I don't like seeing her cry, either."

I nodded. Marco might terrify most people, but I knew him better than that. He was a good man, and he'd never hurt a woman, especially one as innocent and delicate as Ashlyn.

"Did you get her to write the messages?" he prompted.

"Yeah. But I left the notepad in the bedroom.

Maybe wait a while before you go get it. You're right about her needing space."

"Okay, but not too long. We need to send those emails before anyone gets concerned. Her roommate has already texted her phone to check on her. I couldn't unlock the damn thing to answer. We'll need to get her passcode. Did you get her username and password for her email account?"

My lips curved as I recalled the information. Her name was as beautiful as she was, and her password was adorable. "Login is *Abmeyers*. Her password is *Number1unicorn!*"

The corners of Marco's mouth twitched. Coming from him, that was like a delighted laugh. "Cute," he commented.

Ashlyn's bedroom in her apartment at Harvard had been decorated in pastel colors, something between adult sophistication and childish whimsy. I'd known she possessed a girly streak, but the fact that her password was about a magical creature only made her that much more enchanting. Her innocence was something I treasured, something pure that I didn't possess. It was one of the reasons why I wanted to possess *her*.

"I should get going," I said. "I'm supposed to have dinner with my dad at the restaurant, anyway. I'll fill him in on the threat to Ashlyn." My levity melted at the thought of her being threatened. "Maybe he'll agree that it's finally time to make a move against these fuckers."

So far, we'd mostly been engaging in something like a Cold War with my father's rivals. There were moves and countermoves, veiled threats and insults. But outright violence had yet to break out.

"I don't think you should do that," Marco warned. "You can tell him she's here, but don't tell him she's being threatened. Things will get bloody fast, and that could put her in more danger. They were watching her in Cambridge, but if we make a move against them now, they'll know that she's the cause. It'll put a target on her back. They'll know she's our weak spot."

My stomach turned. "Right," I agreed. "I'll keep this between us, but I'll tell Dad that Ashlyn is taking time off from school to stay here with me."

My father wouldn't think it odd that my girlfriend was staying with me at Marco's house. I'd spent enough time here in my life that it wasn't at all out of the ordinary.

"I'll see you later tonight. Take care of her while I'm gone."

"I won't keep the pretty princess locked up alone in her tower, don't worry."

I rolled my eyes at him. I was getting tired of the fairytale jibes.

"I'll make dinner for her," he amended when he could tell I wasn't amused. "And I promise I won't scare her again."

"Thank you." Marco really was good to me, even better than a brother. I knew he'd keep Ashlyn safe and as happy as possible in my absence.

~

My gut tightened with anxiety when I stepped into the back room at Pisolino—my family's restaurant in Manhattan. I'd come to see my father, but Gabriel Costa's deep brown eyes fixed on me, his mouth curving in a cold smile that tugged at the deep scar on his upper lip.

Apparently, even enemies could come together over bucatini all'Amatriciana.

The room was thick with tension. Marco's father, Leo De Luca, sat to Dad's right, as always. And Gabriel, the upstart *capo* who dared to challenge my father, sat at the opposite end of the table.

Dad had been named by Victor Lombardi as his chosen successor, but Gabriel wanted to be the boss, once the old man passed.

"Joseph." My father's voice lacked the usual

warmth he showed me. "Come sit with us. We'll get you a plate."

I tried to remain as nonchalant as possible when I sat to Dad's left. I might not like my violent lifestyle, but the threat to my father rankled. Despite everything, I loved him, and I would die before I let Gabriel Costa hurt him.

"It's always good to see your son, Dominic," Gabriel said to my father. "Family is so important." His dark eyes fixed on me. "It was a shock when you disappeared, Joseph. We were all worried about you."

My father had almost sent men to kill Gabriel while I was hiding out in Cambridge. He'd suspected that his rival had murdered me, and he'd been ready to go to war by the time Marco dragged me back to New York.

"Yes, I'm very happy to have Joseph back where he belongs," Dad said coolly.

Shit. What I had to say wasn't going to go over well with him, but it was actually good that Gabriel was here to hear it. If his people had been thinking about hurting Ashlyn to get to me, I wanted him to know that I had her safely tucked away at Marco's estate, out of their reach.

"Yes, I'm glad to be back." I turned my gaze on my father, but I spoke for Gabriel's benefit. "I don't think I told you about the girl I met in Cambridge,

Dad. Her name is Ashlyn. We missed each other, and I was so worried about her being alone and sad at Harvard." I emphasized *worried*. Dad would get what I was saying. "She's decided to take some time off school to be with me, so she'll be staying at Marco's place for a while. I hope you don't mind if I stay there instead of at home."

I was essentially telling him I wouldn't be in the city to help him with his business for a while, but Dad was sharp enough that he picked up on the veiled significance of my words. Even if I wasn't telling him outright that Ashlyn had been under threat, he could appreciate my caution in bringing her to the safety of the De Luca estate.

"That's great, son," he said with a bland smile that didn't quite reach his eyes. "I hope I can meet her soon."

"I'd like that," I lied. I didn't want Ashlyn anywhere near my mafia family, even my blood relatives.

I'd keep her safely guarded on the estate, with Marco and me. No one would be able to touch her while she was under our protection, especially not Gabriel Costa.

Chapter Sixteen
MARCO

I snuck into my bedroom to retrieve the notepad with Ashlyn's messages. She'd fallen asleep, no doubt exhausted by everything we'd hit her with in the last few hours. Her tears had dried, but I'd waited a long time after her sobbing stopped before I entered the room. I'd been telling Joseph the truth: I didn't like seeing her cry. I might be a monster, but I never hurt women.

Well, I might enjoy delivering a sound spanking when it was warranted, but that would be completely inappropriate. Even if Ashlyn was beautiful enough and bratty enough to make my palm itch to connect with her round ass.

But she belonged to Joseph. And if she was as innocent as he claimed, she wouldn't accept the kinds of games Joseph and I sometimes liked to play with a willing woman. Ashlyn might be our captive, but I wouldn't violate her.

I picked up the notepad from where Joseph had left it on the bed before slipping out of the room, making as little noise as possible. Ashlyn didn't stir, and I was happy for her to get more rest. She'd be more clearheaded once she got some natural sleep and the drugs fully left her system. I'd had to dose her twice to keep her out on the journey to my family's estate. She was probably still feeling some of the effects.

Leaving her safely locked in my bedroom, I went down to the media room and turned on my computer. I usually used it for gaming, but it would do for this more important task.

I accessed the student portal at Harvard and entered Ashlyn's login information to open her email. My lips twitched as I typed *Number1unicorn!* She really was cute. I could see why Joseph had become obsessed with her. The attraction part was easy to understand; Ashlyn was gorgeous. But Joseph had always longed for a simpler, cleaner life than the one we led. Ashlyn might not be simple, but she was certainly pure and innocent in a way no one from our world ever could be.

Yeah, I definitely understood why Joseph wanted her.

When her inbox loaded, I noted a few emails about coursework from professors and one from Jayme, Ashlyn's roommate. She was getting worried that Ashlyn had missed her text, and Jayme couldn't remember seeing her at their apartment last night.

That could easily be explained away, thanks to the roofie I'd slipped her. If Jayme didn't remember much from the previous night, she'd blame it on the strong cocktails she'd downed while we flirted at the bar. She could easily convince herself that she'd seen Ashlyn and simply forgotten about it in her drunken stupor. Jayme would've been confused enough this morning to make that plausible.

I typed out the message Ashlyn had written for her friend, adding a line about how she had seen Jayme sleeping off her hangover on the couch and hadn't wanted to disturb her. The lie Ashlyn had come up with was serviceable: she was on a retreat in Colorado, and she wouldn't have great cell reception there.

That solved the problem of keeping tabs on her text messages. I could turn off her phone altogether, and no one would be suspicious. Not after I finished sending these emails.

The messages to her professors were a little more businesslike, of course. She didn't mention that she was heartbroken, but instead said she'd suffered a personal loss and needed time to grieve. She wrote that she would do her best to keep up with her coursework while she was absent.

That would do.

When I turned the page to find her message to her father, a weight pressed on my chest. The note was tearstained, the ink smudged. I could read her grief as easily as the words on the page.

A strange knot formed in my gut. She must be very close with her father. It probably killed her to lie to him. She'd revealed that she didn't have to check in with her parents every day, but it was obvious that she loved him very much.

Yet another aspect of her life that was as pretty and perfect as she was. Ashlyn had a loving family, a doting father who wouldn't bat an eye at her running off from college and spending money on a fancy retreat.

I'd never wanted for money, but that didn't mean my life remotely resembled hers. My father had given me everything I'd ever demanded from him, mostly to keep me quiet and out of his way. I'd destroyed it all in a childish cry for his attention. That shit had stopped when I wrapped my new Ferrari around a tree at the age of seventeen. He didn't even visit me in the hospital.

At that point, I'd grown up and stopped being an

attention-seeking little pussy.

When I looked down at the tears on Ashlyn's message to her father, something like envy soured my blood, pulsing through my veins before I could fully suppress it.

I shouldn't resent Ashlyn. She hadn't asked to be pulled into our world. She couldn't help that she'd led a charmed life. And why shouldn't she have everything she could possibly want? She'd done nothing to deserve what I'd done to her, stealing her away from her safe, easy life.

I shrugged off my budding sense of guilt.

I wasn't sorry for taking her. Joseph needed her, and I needed Joseph. He was the only family I had in the world. My father might still be alive, but that didn't make him family, not in the ways that counted. Even once I'd dragged Joseph back to New York, he was like a ghost without Ashlyn. He'd never really been happy in his life, but this was on a whole other level. He'd been miserable without her.

So, I'd fixed that.

I'd promised Joseph that Ashlyn would come around and forgive him.

I hoped to hell I hadn't been lying through my teeth.

~

"What do you think you're doing?" I asked, leaning against the doorframe with my arms crossed over my chest. I'd swung the bedroom door open a full thirty seconds ago, and Ashlyn had yet to notice me.

She yelped and jumped away from the drawer she'd been rummaging through. Several more were open, their contents in disarray. I didn't like seeing my neatly organized possessions strewn about, but her blush and guilty expression were cute enough that I could forgive her.

I took a step into the room. She tried to retreat and bumped into the desk behind her.

She held up her hands, as though to reassure me that she wasn't a threat. I almost laughed at the very idea of the curvy little brunette causing me any trouble. She was much smaller than me, and I towered over her. I worked hard to stay fit, keeping my body bulked up. Intimidating people was in my line of work, so being the scariest motherfucker in the room had proven useful on many occasions.

I'd promised Joseph that I wouldn't scare Ashlyn. That didn't mean I wasn't going to indulge in toying with her. The first night I'd met her—when I'd cornered her in the bar where Joseph worked—she'd looked up at me with those wide, blue eyes. She'd quivered in my shadow, and a twisted part of me liked her trepidation. I didn't want to truly frighten her, but I couldn't deny that I liked making her nervous. The effect I had on her was delicious. She might soften and sigh for Joseph, but she'd tremble for me.

I fully acknowledged that she belonged to Joseph. That didn't mean I couldn't have a little fun while he was away. Even if he were here, I didn't think he'd mind. He might be possessive of Ashlyn, but we shared everything. Even women, from time to time.

And while I was certain Ashlyn was far too innocent to contemplate that kind of play, I could toy with her. I could push her. Just a little.

"I asked you a question," I prompted as I slowly advanced on her. "What do you think you're doing, tearing my room apart? It's very rude. Are you being a little brat again?"

Her eyes narrowed, and she lifted her delicate chin in defiance. "Stop saying I'm a brat. You make it sound like I'm a petulant child or something. You freaking *kidnapped* me. I have every right to be angry."

"So, you're tearing through my things because you're angry?" I asked coolly.

I didn't stop advancing on her until mere inches separated our bodies. I didn't make physical contact with her, but I let her feel my presence, pushing into her space enough to make her squirm.

She tried to ease back again, but the desk stopped

her. I pressed my hands to the wood on either side of her hips, trapping her in case she got any wild ideas about bolting for the door. I had a good idea of what she'd been up to in my absence, but I wanted to make her admit her transgressions.

"Tell me what you were doing, Ashlyn," I commanded.

She let out an angry little huff, but her wide eyes watched me warily. "I was looking for a way to contact Jayme, okay?" she said in a rush. "I figured you had to have a spare tablet or something in here."

My brows rose. "Did you really think I'd just leave something like that lying around where you could get your hands on it?"

She licked her lips nervously, and my gaze fixed on her lush mouth. I wondered what she tasted like. Probably like fucking heaven. After all, Joseph did keep calling her his *angel*.

"I expect an answer when I ask you a question," I prompted in my darkest tone.

There it was: the little tremor I'd been waiting for. Her skin pebbled, and her fingers shook. Her pupils dilated, and her head tipped back slightly.

Fuck. I was understanding Joseph's obsession more with every minute I spent with her.

"I..." She took a breath. "I thought it was rhetorical."

"It wasn't."

I stared down at her, waiting for her response, imposing my will on her.

She didn't lower her lashes in a show of submission. Her gaze remained transfixed on mine, as though she couldn't look away.

"I... What did you ask me again?"

A low, rumbling sound left my chest. It took me a moment to recognize it as a laugh.

That was enough to make me ease back. I might be affecting her, but she was entrancing me. I couldn't push too far. She was Joseph's, not mine. And if I stayed this close to her for a second longer, I'd do a whole lot more to keep her trembling for me.

I glanced around at the mess she'd made to give myself an excuse to break eye contact. I noticed my sketchbook in the drawer she'd been going through when I'd walked in. It was still closed.

That was probably for the best. If I'd seen her reaction to my sketches, I couldn't have held back. Because given Joseph's tastes, she'd definitely respond to the images.

"You'll clean this up later," I told her. "Don't go through my things again."

I could move her to one of the sixteen guest bedrooms, but I liked the idea of her sleeping in my bed, even if I couldn't be in there with her. Besides, I had the nicest room in the house, and I didn't intend to treat her badly while she was my captive.

"Come on." I turned and gestured for her to follow me. "I made dinner."

~

"Are you going to keep giving me the silent treatment?" I asked, teasing her just a little. Although she probably wouldn't know I was teasing, since I didn't smile. I rarely did; I didn't have a lot of practice smiling while I was doing my family's work.

Blue sparks danced in her eyes, and the angry twist of her lips let me know she wanted to give me a piece of her mind. She set her fork down beside her nearly empty plate. She'd devoured the spaghetti bolognese I'd made for her, so she must have been hungry. Even if she hadn't commented on my culinary skills, she'd enjoyed it.

"What could we possibly have to talk about?" Her voice was clipped as she flipped her long, dark hair over her shoulder. I wondered if it felt as silky as it looked. I could imagine wrapping it around my fist while she sucked my cock.

My dick throbbed, and I quickly redirected my thoughts.

"You're an Art History major, right? Tell me about that."

She blinked at me. "How do you know I'm an Art History major?"

"I told you, I had people monitoring you. I know a lot about you."

She scowled at me. "You don't know anything about me at all."

"Don't I? I know you have a three point eight two GPA. I know you prefer to wear clothes in pastel colors. I know your favorite coffee shop near campus. I even know that you like your pumpkin spice latte without foam."

Her eyes widened. I'd clearly unsettled her, but there was no point hiding reality from her. This was our world, and she was a part of it now.

"I know your father is a psychiatrist in Savannah, Georgia, and your mother is a neurosurgeon in Chicago. I know they divorced when you were eight, but they both still provided you with enough money for you to have everything you could ever want."

"Shut up!" she shouted with sudden fervor. The hint of fear I'd sensed in her had been overwhelmed by rage. I'd hit a nerve. "You don't know me at all."

She shoved back from the kitchen island where we'd been eating and got to her feet. Without a backward glance at me, she stormed out of the room.

I caught up to her before she got to the foyer. "Where do you think you're going?"

I wrapped my hand around her slender arm when she didn't stop walking. She tried to jerk away, but I held her fast.

"Away from you!" she burst out. "Let me go." She shoved me. When that accomplished nothing, she beat at my chest with her fist.

I didn't even bother catching her wrist to stop her. I simply started walking, keeping my grip on her arm. I was careful not to hold tight enough to bruise, but she had no hope of escaping me.

She was forced to follow, even though she continued to twist her arm in my grip.

"Let me go," she demanded again.

"No. Stop struggling, or you'll hurt yourself."

"*You're* hurting me," she shrieked. She was getting dramatic again. I didn't find her quite as cute anymore.

"No, I'm not. Calm down."

I started leading her toward the stairs.

"Where are you taking me?"

"I'm putting you to bed."

"What?" she spluttered. "You can't do that. I'm not a child."

"You clearly can't behave like a rational adult. If you act like a brat, you get treated like a brat."

"Stop calling me that."

"Stop acting like that."

Her teeth closed with an audible *snap*, and she glowered at me in sullen silence. She also stopped trying to get away from me. She wasn't exactly meek, but she'd definitely gotten the message.

Good. Between her hysterics and Joseph's melodrama, I was ready for this day to be over.

When we got to my room, I finally released her, but I kept her fixed in my stern stare.

I gestured at my overturned bedroom. "I expect this mess to be cleaned up by this time tomorrow," I informed her.

Her jaw dropped, as though she couldn't believe the way I was treating her.

And maybe she couldn't. I was sure she'd been coddled and given everything she'd ever asked for in life. If any girl had ever needed structure and discipline, it was Ashlyn.

She belongs to Joseph, I reminded myself before I got any more ideas about *disciplining* her.

I closed the door, hiding her from my view. I needed to put distance between us, or I might do something I'd regret. I made sure to lock her in before I went back to my media room. I didn't want my little captive to try to escape when I wasn't watching her.

Chapter Seventeen
JOSEPH

"Do you know what your *friend* did to me?" Ashlyn fumed as soon as I opened the bedroom door. She sat on the bed, her arms crossed. She didn't appear to have been engaging in any activity other than stewing over whatever was making her angry.

Marco had told me he locked her in the room over an hour ago. She'd had a lot of time to get worked up.

"He said you were angry after dinner, so he brought you back up here."

She slapped her hand down on the mattress beside her. "He didn't *bring me back up here*. He *put me to bed*. Like I'm some sort of naughty child. He keeps calling me a brat. He's a misogynistic prick."

"He's not," I corrected her, maybe a touch more

sharply than I should have. Marco loved women. In his own way.

She glowered at me. I didn't like when she looked at me like that: like I'd betrayed her. Like she hated me.

I lifted the shopping bags I'd brought with me, a gesture of contrition. "I got some clothes for you in the city."

Her frown eased, and her eyes sparked with interest. She wanted the clothes. I wasn't sure if she simply liked new, pretty things, or if she was desperate to change. She'd been wearing the same clothes since Marco had abducted her last night. That had been over twenty-four hours ago.

I decided I didn't care what the source of her interest was. If she was excited for me to buy her new things, I was happy to give her anything she wanted.

She pointed at the foot of the bed. "You can leave them there," she said in an imperious tone I didn't care for. "I'm going to take a shower."

I didn't move to comply. This haughty attitude didn't suit her softer nature. And it certainly didn't suit me. I'd give her anything she asked for, but if she thought I'd obey her commands, she was sorely mistaken. I might worship her, but that didn't mean I was her slave.

"What?" she asked when I didn't do as she

demanded. She was getting annoyed. "Do I need Marco's *permission* to take a shower or something?"

Something dark stirred in my chest. Because I knew exactly how Marco would feel about her waiting for his permission to do anything. Given the opportunity, he'd probably deny her the shower and insist on bathing her himself. I had my kinks, but Marco possessed his own perversions.

But Ashlyn didn't belong to him. She was mine, and as much as I'd like to join her in the shower, I was very aware of her anger toward me. She wasn't going to forgive me for my complicity in her capture. I wouldn't impose myself on her when she wasn't willing. No matter how badly I might want to.

"You don't need Marco's permission," I informed her coolly. "But that attitude won't get you anywhere with me, either."

Her jaw dropped, but no words came out. I supposed I'd subtly dominated her in the past, but I'd never been overt about it. I could reel myself back now, but I didn't want to. The dark part of me accepted that she was my captive, and I could treat her how I wanted. It was liberating. Something was shifting between us, even if she didn't recognize it yet.

She'd railed at me for hiding my true self from her during our time together in Cambridge.

Well, if she wanted the real me, that's what she'd get. I might not be willing to fully corrupt her with all my perverted desires, but that didn't mean I wasn't going to take her in hand when she was acting this way. Because Marco was right. She was being a brat, acting out in a fit of anger.

She could pout all she wanted, but that wouldn't sway my decision to keep her. She was in danger, and I didn't have a choice. I didn't want the choice. Marco had done me a favor when he brought her to me. I could finally show Ashlyn who I really was, even the ugly parts of myself I wasn't proud of.

I set the shopping bags down and rifled through them, quickly finding what I wanted.

"You can take a shower," I told her. "Here. This is what you're wearing to bed." I held out the short, silky black nightgown I'd bought for her.

Her eyes widened, and her lips parted on an incredulous gasp. I almost groaned at the sight of her shocked, innocent expression. Her open mouth practically begged to take my cock. I'd never felt her lips around me before. I'd always fucked her tight pussy. There were so many other ways I wanted to take her.

"You've worn far less around me," I pointed out when she simply continued to stare at the scrap of black material.

"I didn't... I didn't know you then." She tried to

defy me, but her eyes were still fixed on the nightgown.

"You want to know me? This is me. And you'll do as I say."

Her mouth finally closed, her lips pressing to a thin line. "No. You might be keeping me here against my will, but I don't have to do what you say. You can't boss me around like this."

"Can't I?" I took a step toward her.

She didn't shrink away. She froze where she sat on the bed, her breath catching in her throat.

I'd known she enjoyed a little light sexual domination, but I'd never turned this side of myself on her before. Not really.

I finished closing the distance between us, moving slowly to gauge her reaction. She swallowed, but she didn't recoil.

I reached out and rubbed the silky nightgown against her face, trailing the soft material over her cheek. She drew in a shuddering breath, and her eyes darkened. She didn't flinch from my touch.

"Are you scared, angel? Do I frighten you?"

"No," she breathed, without hesitation. "But I'm mad at you," she added softly. "I don't trust you."

I dropped the nightgown onto the mattress and sat down beside her. She didn't cringe away, so I took her hand in mine.

"I know you don't. But I'll earn your trust back. I promise. I would never do anything to hurt you. All I want to do is keep you safe."

All I want to do is keep you. I'd made sure to add the *safe* part. She'd said she wasn't scared of me, and I didn't want that to change.

She nodded. It might not be a verbal admission that she believed me, but it was a start. I owed her a full explanation for what I was doing to her. I'd wanted so badly to hide my life from her while we'd been together in Cambridge, but that had to change.

"Go take a shower." I softened the command as much as I could manage. "I'll be waiting here, and we'll talk when you come out."

She plucked at the nightgown. "Do I have to wear this?"

I caught her chin between my thumb and forefinger, capturing her in my gaze.

"Does it make you uncomfortable? Do I make you uncomfortable?"

She shifted on the mattress, but I didn't release her.

"A little bit," she admitted.

I raised my free hand to her throat, stroking the column of her neck with my fingertips. She shivered and remained locked in place.

I leaned in to whisper in her ear, and I heard her breathing hitch as I neared.

"Do you want to know a secret, angel? I like making you a little uncomfortable. I like watching you shiver and squirm." I nipped at her earlobe. "Are you scared now?"

"I... No." She tilted her head to the side, giving me better access.

I kissed the hollow beneath her ear before tracing the line of her neck with my tongue. She let out a soft moan. My cock throbbed, but I held myself back. I couldn't fuck her. Not yet. I still owed her the truth, and then she could decide if she was ready to accept me.

"Wear the nightgown for me." I didn't bother to conceal the ring of command this time.

"Okay," she agreed on a sigh.

I would have preferred a *Yes, Sir*, but she was nowhere near ready for that. She might never be ready for that. I craved it, but I could do without if she would be mine.

I pressed a kiss against her collarbone. "Good girl."

I withdrew from her slowly, and she swayed toward me. Our connection was as powerful as ever. She just needed some time and some truth to make her come around and accept it again.

"Go on," I prompted when she didn't move.

She scooted off the bed, grabbing up the scrap of black silk before darting to the opulent bathroom. She shut the door behind her, as though that could put a barrier between us.

It would take a hell of a lot more to truly keep me from her, but for now, I'd give her some breathing room. No matter how badly I wanted to join her in the shower.

～

My cock got rock hard as soon as she stepped out of the bathroom. The skimpy nightgown was so short that it barely covered her pussy. If she turned around, I'd see her luscious ass peeking out beneath the hem.

She stopped in the threshold to the bedroom, freezing in place as I examined her. I allowed myself a full minute to admire her body, drinking in her perfect curves and smooth, alabaster skin. Her nipples pebbled in response to my rapt attention, and the thin silk did little to hide the peaked buds.

I wanted to close the distance between us and rip the flimsy material from her body, revealing the dusky pink tips of her nipples and exposing her fully. It had been so long since I'd seen her naked, and I ached to learn her perfection all over again.

Her teeth sank into her pouty lower lip, and her hands twisted together in front of her. I recognized her nervous tics. She was feeling shy, vulnerable.

Now wasn't the time for me to strip her, pin her against the wall, and fuck her hard. She needed me to handle her carefully; she needed tenderness, not aggression. I found her innocence enticing, but I didn't want her to be anxious around me.

I stood and approached her slowly, allowing her time to move away if she wanted to.

She remained fixed in place. Her eyes roved over my body as I moved, flicking down from my steady stare to focus on the ridge of my cock where it strained against my jeans. She licked her lips, and I bit back a lustful growl.

When I reached her, I took a deep breath and held out my hand, giving her the option to take it.

She immediately initiated contact, clasping my hand with her much smaller one. I closed my fingers around hers and led her back to the bed, guiding her to sit beside me on the edge of the mattress.

I brushed a stray lock of hair back from her face, and she closed her eyes at the electric contact. I didn't want to stop touching her, so I indulged myself. I stroked her hair, letting the damp, dark chocolate strands fall through my fingers. When I reached her shoulder, I traced the line of her collarbone before running my palm down her arm. Her skin pebbled beneath my touch, her body lighting up with the same awareness that gripped me.

My fingers closed around her hand again, my thumb brushing across the inside of her wrist. Her eyes closed, and she swayed toward me. Her head tipped back, waiting for my lips to capture hers.

I brought my free hand up and allowed it to sink into her hair, fisting it at her nape. She sucked in a small gasp when I tugged her back, and her eyes flew wide.

I thought I'd see the sting of rejection in her eyes, and an apology teased at the tip of my tongue. But it wasn't necessary. She stared up at me with raw lust. She liked my hand in her hair, the little bite of pain as I wrapped it around my fist and took control.

With great effort, I eased my hold and resumed stroking her, lightly massaging her scalp.

She let out a blissful sigh and leaned toward me again. She wasn't seeking a kiss this time. She rested her head against my shoulder, relaxing into me.

I shifted my touch just long enough to grip her waist and position her body so she was curled up in my lap. Then, I resumed petting her. She snuggled closer with a happy humming sound.

"I missed you, angel," I said, my voice a pleased rumble.

"I missed you too," she admitted. She lifted her head, her beautiful blue eyes catching mine. "You said we could talk. I'm still not happy with you, but I want to hear what you have to say."

I lightly rubbed a pressure point behind her ear, and her lashes fluttered as she practically purred.

I chuckled. "Are you sure you're not happy, angel?"

"Stop distracting me and talk," she grumbled, but there was no real bite in the order.

I took a deep, sobering breath. It was time to discuss the reality of her situation, and that knowledge cooled most of my lust. Once I was finished, she might turn from me in disgust.

But I'd never earn her trust again if I wasn't honest with her. I needed her trust; I craved it. The feel of her softening beneath me as she gave me everything was too addictive. I'd risk anything to have that back.

"I'm not a good man," I murmured. "I'm not, but I wanted to be."

I still wanted it, but now that I'd been dragged back to my violent life, I knew that was just a childish dream.

"That's why I ran away to Cambridge," I continued. "I wanted to start over, to have a simpler life. I thought I could have that with you, but instead, I pulled you into my world. And I'm sorry for that."

She stared up at me, hopeful. "So, you are sorry for kidnapping me?"

"I'm sorry I put you in danger. But no, I'm not sorry that Marco brought you to me." Raw honesty was the only way forward. "I want you, Ashlyn. I need you with me. I was a fucking mess without you."

"I wasn't doing great without you, either" she admitted. "I want to be with you, but not like this. Can't we just go back to Cambridge? I'm scared, Joseph. Marco said you're involved with the mafia, and he said your enemies... He said they'd hurt me." A small tremor ran through her body.

Damn Marco for scaring her. He'd been trying to talk some sense into her, but he'd been too blunt. I never would've told her the fucked-up things our enemies might do to her if they caught her. I wanted to shield her from that fear.

"We can't go back," I told her, the words acid on my tongue. I wished we could, but I wouldn't be able to protect her there. Not by myself. The dream of sharing a normal life with her was shattered beyond repair, and all I could do was let it go. Marco was right: this was our reality. Ashlyn and I both had to face it.

"I am sorry for that, but I'll do whatever it takes to keep you safe. Even if it means you hate me for keeping you here, I'll do it."

"I...I don't hate you. I don't think I'm capable of hating you."

Relief surged through me, a pulse of light through my entire body.

She doesn't hate me. It wasn't the same as trusting me, but it was a start. I'd earn her trust back. It would just take time. She'd adjust and accept her place here with me. It might never be possible for her to return to her old life. Even if we dealt with my father's enemies and the immediate danger passed, she was in my world now.

I didn't like the world I lived in, but it would be bearable with Ashlyn in my arms.

"I'm everything Marco said I am," I told her. "I'm all that and worse. Like I said, I'm not a good man. But I'll be good to you. I'll take care of you, just like I did in Cambridge. I hid my past from you, but that part of me was never a lie. All I want is to take care of you. I know you don't want to be here, but I'm still going to try to make you happy. Will you give me a chance to do that?"

Her eyes were tight with longing. She wanted everything I promised. She wanted to be sheltered and adored.

She just didn't want to be my captive.

"I want to go back to school," she begged. "Please, take me back. And stay there with me."

Maybe Marco had been right to be so blunt with her. She still wasn't fully grasping the danger she faced.

"I wish I could give you what you want, but I can't. I can't make any promises about taking you back. I can't let you go. I won't."

Ashlyn was mine, and it was time she acknowledged it. She already belonged to me. I could feel it in the way she leaned into me for comfort even as she begged me to release her. This might not be the way she wanted our relationship to go, but at least we were together. My life had been hell without her, and I wasn't sorry for keeping her.

I'd just have to remind her how good it could be between us.

I shifted my hand in her hair so I grasped her nape, and I pulled her toward me to finally capture her lips.

Fuck, I'd forgotten how good she tasted—pure sin from the mouth of an angel.

I'd licked at the salt of her tears this morning, but those were apologetic kisses, meant to soothe.

I didn't want to soothe her now. I wanted to consume her.

As soon as her lips parted for me, my tongue surged into her mouth on a hungry growl. My other hand eased up her thigh, the reverent touch contrasting with the almost brutal way I claimed her lips. I nipped at them, kissing her hard enough to make them swollen.

Good. I wanted her to bear marks of my possession. I might not be able to mark her skin like I truly wanted, but I could allow myself this one dark pleasure. I knew my sweet, pure angel was far too innocent for all the kinky things I wanted to do to her, so I'd hold back.

Mostly.

My fingers dipped beneath the hem of the silk nightgown, and I found her lower lips were swollen, too. She was slick and ready for me. I brushed my thumb over her clit. It was hard, needy. She mewled into my mouth, and I devoured the sound.

I withdrew from her pussy and palmed her breasts, re-learning their weight and shape before memorizing the perfection of her peaked nipples.

It still wasn't enough. I could feel her through the silk, but I needed to see her.

I tore my mouth from hers, and she made a little sound of protest. Her hands curled into my shoulders, and she tried to pull me closer.

She'd never been a match for my strength. I loved how delicate and fragile she felt in my hands. I might kiss her roughly, but I handled her with aching care.

I guided her down onto her back, stretching her

out on the bed beneath me. I placed her arms above her head, squeezing her wrists gently to reinforce my control.

"Don't move," I ordered. I was already riding the intoxicating high I got off even this light domination. She was so fucking beautiful in her willing submission to me. She stared up at me with her big blue eyes, her breathing coming fast and shallow. I released her wrists, and her arms remained above her head.

Perfect.

I fisted the silky nightgown in both hands. With one jerk of my arms, the thin material ripped down the middle. The savage tearing sound mingled with my primal growl. I was getting lost in her, drunk on my power over her.

Her wide eyes told me she was shocked by my aggressive actions, but her body reacted beautifully. She gasped and arched her back, thrusting her exposed breasts up to silently beg for my touch.

I settled my weight over her hips, ensuring she was pinned beneath me. She moaned and arched again, struggling to get her nipples closer to my mouth.

I gave her what she wanted, licking the tight buds before gently sucking them. Her head thrashed against the pillow, but she didn't move her hands in an effort to hold me against her.

I wedged my thigh between her legs, and she rotated her hips, grinding against me. Her wetness marked my jeans. She was eager, desperate.

And so was I.

I couldn't take the time to get undressed, so I pushed aside the urge to feel her skin sliding against mine. I could indulge that desire that later. Right now, I needed to get inside her more than I needed my next breath.

I reached into Marco's nightstand drawer and grabbed a condom. Ashlyn watched me, her eyes wild and needy. I bit back a curse and freed my cock from my jeans and boxers, sheathing myself before lining up with her slick opening.

I leaned over her, pressing her deeper into the mattress with my weight. She squirmed beneath me, rubbing herself against me like a needy kitten. But she still didn't move her arms from above her head.

"Such a good girl," I praised, brushing her hair back from her cheek. "Are you ready for me, angel?"

"Yes," she panted. "Please, Joseph. I need you."

I sank my fingers into her hair, tightening my grip around the lustrous strands as I tipped her head back for a ruthless kiss. She cried out into my mouth when I thrust into her at the same time.

Her inner walls contracted around me, struggling to take to my size after a month of emptiness. My lips firmed around hers as I struggled to control myself. I stilled within her, allowing her time to adjust. I should have kissed her more gently, coaxing her. But I couldn't. Need drove me to the edge of sanity, and I couldn't be as careful with her as I'd been in the past.

Her muscles finally began to relax around me. Shock tore through me when my little innocent angel wrapped her legs around my hips and dug her heels into my ass, pulling me deeper.

I groaned against her and pulled almost all the way out before driving back into her, hard enough to rock her body beneath mine. She moved with me, drawing me in to the hilt. Animal instinct took over, and I snarled into her mouth. She moaned and opened for me, her tongue dancing with mine.

She hadn't tried to move her hands, but I curled my fingers around her wrists and pinned them against the pillow. I needed to feel her trapped beneath me, writhing and whimpering as I took her, hard and relentless. She screamed out her orgasm, the sound of her pleasure vibrating into my mouth.

I didn't want to finish with her just yet, but too much time had passed without her in my life. Her ecstasy triggered mine, and I came undone on a shout, driving into her without finesse as I rode my release. Her pussy fluttered around me with the aftershocks of her own orgasm. She went limp beneath me, exhausted and sated.

I finally broke our kiss and gasped out a curse as the last of my orgasm faded. I rolled off her, but I pulled her with me so she was draped over my chest.

"I missed you so much," she murmured against my neck.

I didn't have words heavy enough to express how empty I'd been without her, how happy I was to have her back in my arms.

I captured her lips again, kissing her slow and deep this time. If I couldn't tell her how I felt, I'd show her.

Chapter Eighteen
ASHLYN

Joseph collapsed beside me, breathing hard. I rolled with him, keeping him inside me. He'd just given me yet another explosive orgasm, but I wasn't ready to be parted from him. When we'd had sex last night, he hadn't taken off his clothes. I'd needed him too desperately to care about it then, but now, I definitely appreciated his naked body.

He was even harder and bulkier than I remembered. I wasn't certain what he did with his days—I had no clue what it meant to be a mobster—but whatever he did, it required more physical exertion than bartending. I'd thought he was massive and muscular when I'd first met him, but now he was impossibly more ripped. His abs flexed against me as I trailed my fingernails over them, memorizing the way his muscles rippled and danced beneath my light touch.

I explored further, running my palm over his hard chest and down his corded arm, feeling his strength. His masculine perfection was enough to make my mouth water and my pussy clench. He grunted as my inner walls contracted around his cock.

"You shouldn't do that, angel," he warned.

"Why not?" I squeezed again, and he groaned. He began to stiffen inside me, even though we'd just finished a few minutes ago. Knowing I had this effect on him made a sense of feminine power course through me.

He chuckled, low and dark. He shifted, withdrawing from me so he could manhandle me into position. He grasped my ankles and guided them up to rest against his shoulders before he moved over me. His weight forced my thighs close to my chest, spreading me wide for him. He gripped my wrists and pinned them at either side of my head. We'd played a few games like this back in Cambridge, but he was different now. More demanding. Less restrained.

My pussy wept for him, swelling and growing slick in response to the way he handled my body.

A sharp knock on the door made me yelp, shattering the moment. Joseph wasn't in any particular rush to roll off me, and I barely managed to get my legs down and jerk the sheet over my body before the door opened.

I gaped at Marco where he stood at the threshold.

"Close the door!" I demanded, pulling the sheet up to my chin.

His heavy brows rose. "It's my bedroom."

"Joseph," I said sharply, looking over at him. I expected him to come to my defense and throw his overbearing friend out.

He didn't appear upset in the slightest. He'd almost beaten a guy for grabbing my arm once, but he'd allow his friend to walk in on us when we were about to have sex?

"What?" he asked his friend, but he still didn't sound aggressive or even annoyed.

"I made breakfast," Marco told him. "Finish up and come down, or it'll get cold."

A little noise of disbelief huffed from my chest when he sauntered off, not bothering to close the door behind him.

"What the hell?" I asked, looking back to Joseph. "You almost ripped Stu apart for touching me at the bar in Cambridge, but you let your best friend ogle me?"

"He wasn't ogling you. He came to tell us he made breakfast."

"I'm *naked*," I reminded him, wondering what had happened to my fierce, possessive protector.

He gave me a lopsided smile. "And you pulled the covers up high enough that he could barely see your face. Marco won't touch you, Ashlyn. You don't need to be afraid of him."

I scoffed. Of course I was afraid of him. Marco was even more heavily muscled than Joseph, and he lacked any kindness in his hard black eyes. The only times I'd ever seen him look remotely amused, it had been at my expense.

"Hey," Joseph said, more gently. He took my hand in his. "I know he scared you yesterday, but Marco was just trying to help. He was trying to make you understand that he brought you here for your own good. We want to protect you. Both of us."

I searched his face, studying him. He seemed completely sincere, but I wasn't certain that he had an accurate view of his friend's true nature. There was something dark about Marco, something deep in his soul. Joseph hated his life of violence—he'd made that much clear—but Marco didn't seem at all bothered by it. He probably thrived on it.

"I want you to come back to Cambridge with me," I announced. "After, I mean," I said before he could start lecturing me about his enemies again.

"After the danger has passed, I want to go back to school, and I want you to come with me."

Something shifted in his eyes, but the shadow was gone so fast, I was sure I must have imagined it.

He brushed a kiss against my forehead. "I'd like that, angel."

"Good. Then I'll stay here with you. I can take a little time off school, as long as I try to keep up with my coursework. I don't suppose Marco grabbed my books when he abducted me?" I asked, although I knew that was highly unlikely.

"He didn't, but I'll buy new editions for you. Can you access your syllabi online?"

"Yes. I just need the textbooks so I can follow along with the assignments. If I can send another email to my professors, I'll ask if someone will volunteer to upload their class notes for me. Would that be okay?" I didn't like asking for permission, but I doubted I'd be granted access to the internet. I didn't believe for one second that Marco would trust me near a computer, no matter that I had decided to stay without complaint.

"Of course," Joseph agreed easily. "Just write out the message, and Marco will send the email. I'll order your books online today. We can go over what you need after breakfast." He gave me a crooked smile that made my heart melt. "We really should go downstairs. Marco gets cranky if his food goes cold."

"Why doesn't he just eat without us?"

I followed Joseph out of bed and went through the shopping bags he'd brought me last night, looking for something to wear.

"He probably won't wait for us, but he doesn't like when his culinary creations aren't enjoyed properly."

I shot him an incredulous glance. "Marco doesn't strike me as the type who would care about something like that."

"I think you have the wrong impression of him. Marco likes cooking for people. It's one of his hobbies."

"If you say so," I allowed. I couldn't imagine Marco caring enough about anyone to worry what they thought of his cooking.

I kept searching through the bags, but I couldn't find what I was looking for.

"Where are the bras and underwear?" I asked.

Joseph's smile turned wolfish. "There aren't any."

"I can't go around without a bra," I said, aghast at the thought of my nipples poking through the thin camisoles he'd gotten for me.

"Yes, you can. There's no one here to see." He stepped toward me, wrapping his arm around my waist and pulling me close so he could whisper in my ear. "I want access to your body at all times. Does it bother you that I want to be able to fuck you without panties getting in the way? If I'd gotten them for you, I'd just end up ripping them off. That would be a waste, don't you think?"

"But...Marco's here," I spluttered.

"He'll be fine."

"I don't want him looking at me." Marco made me uncomfortable. He liked to get in my personal space. He liked intimidating me. I could see it in the way emotion sparked in his eyes when he got close to me. At all other times, he appeared almost bored, detached. But when he made me squirm, pleasure stirred in his dark gaze. It was beyond unnerving.

"Then I'll tell him not to look," Joseph promised, as though that settled it. "Now, get dressed. I don't want Marco getting pissy."

"But I..."

"Now, Ashlyn." He fixed me with a stern stare he'd never turned on me before.

I was pulling on the camisole and yoga pants before I fully processed my actions. I wasn't scared of Joseph, but that deeper note in his voice warned me not to defy him. I wasn't sure what would happen if I did, but I didn't even think about testing him.

When I was dressed, the stern expression melted, replaced by a dazzling smile that knocked the air from my chest. He planted a swift kiss on my lips and took my hand in his, leading me out of the bedroom.

I finally had a chance to look around the house a little as we made our way to the kitchen; I'd been too emotional last night to really take it in. Well, *house* wasn't an accurate word. From the little bit I'd seen, Marco lived in a mansion, with enough white marble and gold gilding to make it look like an Italian palace. The effect was ostentatious, and that didn't fit with the no-nonsense vibe I'd gotten from Marco.

"This is really Marco's house?" I asked as Joseph kept step beside me, holding my hand as we made our way down the elegant curved staircase. On the way down, we passed a low-hanging chandelier with enough dripping crystals to throw rainbows onto the domed ceiling. I glanced up and noted the painted fresco above us. The art historian in me was interested, but I was still puzzled by the fact that Marco had cherubs depicted on his ceiling.

"It's his father's house," Joseph told me. "But Leo rarely comes here. Marco has had the place to himself for most of his life."

That sounded kind of lonely. "What about his mother? Doesn't he have any siblings?"

Joseph's expression shuttered. "That's for Marco to tell you, if he wants to."

I wanted to ask why it was such a secret, but deep

in my heart, I understood. I didn't want people knowing about my estrangement from my mother, either. It was so much easier to plaster on a smile and talk about what a great surgeon she was, how proud I was of her achievements. When in reality, all I felt was resentment and abandonment.

"Oh. Okay." I let the subject drop, but I would never ask Marco about it. I didn't want to be anywhere near him, much less have heart-to-hearts about our families. Besides, I wasn't sure if Marco even had a heart.

When we got to the kitchen, Marco was nowhere to be seen. Two perfect, fluffy omelets were plated and waiting on the marble-topped island. Joseph pulled out one of the barstools for me, treating me with the same gentlemanly consideration he'd always shown me when we were together in Cambridge. It seemed that part of him had been genuine.

Last night, he'd said he wanted to protect me and make me happy. I believed him, even if my mind was still reeling from the revelations about his lifestyle. It would take time for me to fully accept that my sweet Joseph was a criminal, but the fact that he'd tried to escape and make a new, better life for himself made it easier to swallow. If we just waited until the danger passed, we could go back to Cambridge together. He could start over. I could go back to my life, and Joseph would be at my side.

The knowledge made it much easier to accept my situation. Marco might have kidnapped me, but I wasn't a captive here. Not really. Joseph was just trying to shelter me and keep me safe. It would be foolish to reject his protection.

And I wasn't certain that he would give me the option to reject it. A part of me recognized that the dynamic between us might be very different if I'd continued to defy his decision to keep me here.

I remembered the way he'd wrapped his hand around my throat, pinning me down and kissing my desperate tears. I'd never seen that side of him before. It made my stomach drop and my pulse race.

"I guess Marco already ate," Joseph said, breaking into my dark thoughts. He touched two fingers beneath my chin, redirecting my gaze to his. "You okay, angel?"

"Yeah," I answered, and it was the truth. When he was looking at me with soft concern, touching me with such gentleness, I couldn't be frightened of him. "I'm just hungry."

He grinned. "Then we'd better eat before it gets cold."

The eggs had already cooled a bit while we'd lingered in the bedroom, so I ate them quickly before they got rubbery. The omelet was delicious, just the right consistency and stuffed with bacon and cheese. Apparently, Marco really did enjoy cooking. It seemed like a weird hobby for a ruthless criminal, but I supposed even mobsters had to eat.

Although, given the opulence of his mansion, I suspected Marco's family could afford a live-in chef.

I shrugged off my curiosity, deciding I didn't really care what Marco liked to do with his free time when he wasn't intimidating people and committing horrible crimes.

"Do you want to see the rest of the grounds?" Joseph asked when I set down my fork, my plate completely cleaned. It really had been delicious.

"Sure." It would be nice to go outside. I'd spent most of yesterday sleeping, and when I'd woken up, it had been dark. Before my futile attempt to discover a tablet to access the internet and get a message to Jayme, I'd checked out the window as a possible escape route. Floodlights had illuminated the brick walkway below, at least a two-story drop. I'd definitely break something if I attempted to escape that way.

Other than that, I hadn't been able to make out much more than a grassy expanse that disappeared into darkness.

I no longer intended to escape, but I'd still like to

check out my surroundings. If I couldn't leave this place, I might as well become familiar with my gilded cage. Because no matter Joseph's good motives in keeping me here, I was still restricted to the confines of this estate for the foreseeable future.

I shook off the thought before the sensation of being trapped could set in. This wasn't a cage; it was a refuge.

Joseph took my hand again, and all my worry melted away. I walked with him out of the kitchen, across the foyer, and out the front door.

It was a chilly autumn day, and goosebumps instantly broke out on my exposed skin. I was only wearing the thin camisole Joseph had bought for me, and my peaked nipples pressed against the fabric in response to the cold.

To my surprise, Joseph frowned and rubbed my arms, his eyes focused on my face rather than my breasts. He was more concerned with my comfort than checking out my tits. The knowledge that he cared more about seeing to my needs than satisfying his own lust for my body made warmth flood my chest.

"I'll get you a jacket," he said, guiding me back into the foyer to shield me from the cold. "Wait here."

I hugged my arms across my chest when he

retreated, a chill lingering on my skin. A light shiver wracked my body, but he returned in less than a minute. He held his leather jacket, and he stepped behind me so I could slip my arms into it. The leather was heavy on my shoulders, the jacket far too big for my much smaller frame. It smelled like Joseph, and I breathed in deeply as he zipped it up to keep me warm.

"Thanks." I smiled, completely content in this moment with him. When he took care of me like this, I couldn't worry about the dark events unfolding around me. I knew he would do more than keep me safe; he'd cherish me. The knowledge was heady, and pleasure washed through my body in a tingling wave.

He traced the line of my jaw, staring down at me with open adoration. "You are so beautiful," he murmured before he pressed a quick, sweet kiss against my lips.

I flushed as my pleasure intensified. This was more than the physical ecstasy that his touch elicited from my body; this was a soul-deep satisfaction that I'd only ever felt with him.

Despite everything that was happening—despite the horrible truths I'd learned about him—I was still infatuated. I wasn't ready to fully trust him yet, but my heart still yearned for his affection.

I kept the love locked in my chest, not willing to

voice it aloud yet. I needed to know more about the real Joseph before I could fully open my heart to him again. Trust had never come easily for me, and he'd violated it by hiding his past from me. It would take time for him to earn it back.

He wrapped his arm around my waist, pulling me close to his body heat as we walked out onto the grounds. A long, paved driveway cut through an expansive lawn, the asphalt disappearing into a line of trees. I started to walk down it, but Joseph steered me closer to the house.

"There's nothing that way," he told me. "The gate is just a few minutes' drive through the tree line. There's an electric fence around the entire estate, and Marco will be alerted if anyone tries to breach it. No one is allowed in without his permission."

The information was baffling, totally at odds with the world I knew. This wasn't just a house; it was a fortress. Hearing about the security made me more aware of the dangerous life Joseph led, but it also made me breathe a little easier. No one could get to me here.

We walked around the house—which took a considerable amount of time due to its sprawling expanse. Marco might as well live in a castle, complete with elaborate gardens. I spotted a large garage to the side of the house. One of the multiple doors was open, and I noted a couple of motorcycles and a red sports car. I didn't know much about cars, but I could tell it was expensive, just like everything else on this estate.

Apparently, crime paid.

When we reached the back of the mansion, excitement fizzed in my chest. Through the windows that enclosed the conservatory, I could see a covered indoor pool.

"Oh!" I exclaimed. "Can I go swimming while I'm here?"

"You like to swim?"

I supposed I'd neglected my morning laps during my time with Joseph in Cambridge. I'd been too attached to him to take time to go to the pool.

"Yeah. I was on the swim team in high school. I usually swim laps every day." Not only was it good exercise, but it helped me clear my head and relax, centering me at the beginning of my day.

"I'll talk to Marco about getting the pool serviced, then. It's been drained and covered for as long as I can remember."

"Really? Why?"

I couldn't imagine having the luxury of an indoor pool in my own home but not using it.

Joseph's expression went smooth. "You'd have to ask Marco."

Another mystery only Marco could answer. Again, I decided I didn't care much, as long as I had access to the pool.

"Will you buy me some swimsuits?" I asked, fully confident that Joseph would follow through on his promise.

He shot me a wicked smile. "I didn't buy you underwear. Do you really think I'm going to buy you swimsuits?"

I let out a huff of disbelief. It was one thing to walk around with my nipples poking through my shirt. It was another to be completely naked in Marco's house.

"Marco might see me," I reminded him.

"You seem very concerned about that."

My cheeks flamed. "Of course I am. I don't like him."

Joseph's smile melted. "I know he intimidated you. And I know it must have been scary when he abducted you. But he would never hurt you, I promise."

I wasn't sure I could fully believe it. "That doesn't mean I'm okay with him seeing me naked." I countered. The fact that Joseph didn't share this viewpoint was bizarre. I understood that—despite having completely different personalities—Marco and Joseph were best friends. What I didn't understand was why Joseph didn't seem as possessive of me around him as he had been back in Cambridge. Had his protective behavior been a carefully crafted lie to make me trust him?

Joseph's eyes searched my face, reading my displeasure.

"Okay, angel," he allowed, his tone contrite. "I'll get you swimsuits. I don't want you to be unhappy here."

I breathed a small sigh of relief. If he'd refused, there would have been nothing I could do about it. It sank in that I was completely reliant on him for everything as long as I was trapped here.

I'm not trapped. He's keeping me here because it's the safest place for me. I'm choosing to stay until the danger passes.

Despite my rationalization, my unease lingered until Joseph swept me up in a mind-numbing kiss. I fell into his arms, forgetting all my worries.

Chapter Nineteen
ASHLYN

I surveyed Marco's bedroom when I stepped out of the bathroom, my hair damp from the shower I'd just taken. The room was a mess, Marco's belongings still strewn about from my frantic search for a tablet the night before.

I expect this mess to be cleaned up by this time tomorrow. His stern words echoed in my head. I still internally balked at being ordered around like an unruly child, but I didn't dare test Marco. If he told me to clean up the room, I'd clean it up. Besides, I had been the one to make the mess, and it was his room I'd torn apart.

I wondered why he was even letting me stay in his bedroom, but I decided it didn't matter. Maybe he liked one of the other bedrooms in the house better. It wasn't really any of my concern.

What I was concerned with was getting the room tidy before meeting Joseph downstairs for dinner. After spending the afternoon cuddling on the couch and binge-watching *Stranger Things*, he'd told me he needed to take a phone call from his father. I'd decided to take a shower while he talked to his dad, and I hoped Marco wasn't around when I did go down to meet Joseph for dinner. I really didn't like being near him, so I hoped he ate his dinner and left before I arrived in the kitchen.

But first, I had to clean up the mess I'd made. Before I'd tossed Marco's things around the room, it had been neat as a pin, everything organized and in an orderly place. Even his pencils were carefully laid out in a neat row in the top drawer, each one sharpened to a perfect point. Why one person needed so many pencils, I didn't understand.

It didn't matter why he had them; all that mattered was that I put them back into their orderly little row. I'd also thrown several books around—mostly biographies. I put them back on the bookshelf where they belonged, even placing them in alphabetical order by author when I realized the pattern of the books that remained on the shelf. I didn't want Marco to be able to accuse me of doing a bad job at cleaning up. I didn't want him to have any reason to get all intimidating and insert himself in my space again.

When the books were back in order, I returned to the desk. I put some notepads back in place on the polished mahogany surface before moving to shut the drawers I'd nearly yanked out of the desk altogether in my desperation.

My eyes caught on a large, leather-bound book that had been hidden in one of the drawers. It was soft to the touch, the forest green leather worn from extensive handling. There weren't any markings on the cover, and it seemed too large to be one of Marco's numerous non-fiction titles that he stored on the bookshelf.

Curiosity urged me to pick up the book and flip it open.

My heart stuttered.

The leather cover didn't conceal an obscure biography or novel. This was a sketchbook. And the first sketch was...unsettling.

Perverted.

Dirty.

Wrong.

The lead pencil strokes were light, as soft and elegant as the woman portrayed in the drawing. As a work of art, it was breathtaking. But what really stole my breath was the subject of the drawing. The woman was naked, her back arched and her lips parted on a silent cry. Her expression was one of ecstasy: her eyes were closed, and the lines of her face were drawn with erotic tension. Her breasts were thrust out, her nipples peaked.

But her nudity was the least disturbing part of the drawing. Twisted strands of rope were wrapped around her body, framing her breasts and putting them on lewd display. Her arms were drawn tight behind her, forcing her back to arch toward the artist. She was on her knees, her thighs spread wide to reveal her bare sex.

After several long minutes, I turned the page, trying to replace the image that was burned into my mind. My breath caught. There was another bound woman. She was different—her hair darker, her nose slightly smaller, and her chin more pointed. Both women were beautiful, but unique.

I flipped the page again. Another woman, her body twisted by the rope that bound her. Her mouth was open on a silent scream, and I was unsure if it was one of pleasure or pain.

Transfixed, I continued to flip through the book, finding sketch after lewd sketch. I tried to appreciate the artist's skill, but all I could focus on were the women, their faces contorted in various states of erotic expression. Some were serenely blissful, others shouting out. I couldn't tell if those women were screaming for pleasure or for mercy, and that unsettled me more than anything.

I was about a third of the way through the book when I gasped. This woman wasn't bound. She wasn't naked. It was a close-up portrait of her face. Her dark hair contrasted with her pale skin. Her irises were nearly black, almost swallowed by her dilated pupils. Her eyes were so wide that her long lashes brushed her brows, and her full lips were parted on a gasp that mirrored my own.

It wasn't just the look of shock, the hint of fear in her eyes, that resembled my current state. I was looking at myself.

"That's you, on the night I met you."

I yelped and nearly jumped out of my skin at the sound of Marco's deep voice. His massive body filled the open doorway, and his black eyes studied me with keen interest.

"I went to that dive bar in Cambridge, looking for Joseph so I could bring him home," he continued. "I found you there. My people who'd tracked him down told me he had a girlfriend. I knew if I confronted you, Joseph would come straight for me."

He stepped into the room, but I couldn't move away. I was frozen, locked in place by his dark stare. My breathing came fast and shallow as he approached. He didn't stop until mere inches separated our bodies. Just like on the night we'd met, he leaned over me, his powerful aura bearing down on me. My heart hammered in my chest, signaling that I should flee.

But I couldn't move. My feet were rooted to the floor, and my fingers were going numb around the leather binding of the sketchpad.

Marco's sketchpad. His drawings. His darkness, put down on paper in lurid detail.

One corner of his lips twitched. "You were so pretty, with your wide, big blue eyes. Like a frightened doe. I understood why Joseph had become obsessed with you." He gestured at the book. "Turn the page, curious little girl. You know you want to."

"I don't," I squeaked. "I didn't mean to pry. I—"

"Turn. The. Page."

My fingers flicked to the next page before I could think of protesting. His darkness pulsed around me, lighting up my body with awareness of his nearness.

"Look," he commanded.

"I don't want to," I whispered. "I don't want to see any more. I'm sorry I—"

"Look." The word cracked through the air like a whip, and my eyes flicked down to the page.

My entire body flushed, and my heart fluttered in

my chest. My stomach did a funny flip, and my mouth went dry.

It was another drawing of me. But this time, I was naked. Bound with rope.

And Joseph was standing behind me, holding the coil as he wrapped it around my body.

"What..." I gasped for air. "What is this?"

"It's you and Joseph, obviously."

My heart leapt into my throat, and I tried to swallow it down so I could speak. "He wouldn't... He'd never..."

Marco made a soft humming noise, considering. "So, he hasn't tied up his pretty little princess? Does he not want to pervert his perfect angel?"

Angel. Joseph's sweet name for me was heavy with mockery.

"This is... You're..." I couldn't find the words to express my feelings. They were jumbled, my emotions roiling. I was too hot; I was practically panting. Marco was far too close, and his body heat was stifling.

"There's that pretty blush," he observed, his voice thick with pleasure I'd never heard from him. "You are innocent, aren't you?"

I wasn't blushing. I was burning up. I had to get away from Marco before the inferno engulfed me.

The sketchbook slipped from my hands, and I

darted past Marco, gasping for fresh air as I rushed through the bedroom door. His low, dark chuckle followed me out into the hall and down the stairs.

When I burst into the kitchen, I flung my arms around Joseph, looking to him for the protection he'd promised. He cradled me against his strong body, holding me with care.

"What's wrong, angel?"

"Marco. He..." I took a deep breath. I couldn't bring myself to tell Joseph about what I'd seen. It was too lewd, too embarrassing. The image of Joseph looming behind me holding the coil of rope burned in my mind. "You'd never...hurt me, right?"

"Of course not." He curled two fingers beneath my chin, lifting my face to his. "Did Marco say something that scared you again?"

I bit my lip. I'd been the one to pry into his privacy and look at his sketches. Marco had every right to be angry at me for that.

But he hadn't been angry. He'd been... I wasn't sure how to describe the thick atmosphere that had built around us as he loomed over me, commanding me to look at the perverted depiction of me with Joseph. Why would he draw something like that?

I didn't answer Joseph's question directly. I simply hugged him tighter.

"I don't like him," I whispered.

"Marco won't hurt you," he promised. "And I won't, either. I'd never hurt you, Ashlyn. All I want is for you to be safe and happy."

I nodded against his chest, knowing he fully believed what he was saying about his dangerous friend. I wasn't at all certain that I was safe around Marco. He made my belly quiver and my pulse race.

"Stay with me?" I pleaded, not wanting to leave Joseph's side with Marco in the house.

"I'm right here," he reassured me, stroking his hand up and down my back. "I've got you."

With that promise, I finally relaxed into his strong arms, knowing deep in my soul that he would protect me.

Chapter Twenty
JOSEPH

"If you're down here, I'm guessing she's still asleep," Marco said as I joined him in the kitchen for breakfast. "You can't even leave her for five seconds while she's conscious. You two are kind of nauseating in real life."

"What do you mean *in real life?*"

He shrugged. "When I sent people to find you, they took pictures of you together. You looked happy. Then, once you came back home, I saw how you were without her. You were completely fucked up. I thought bringing her here would make you happy again."

"I am happy," I said, not really understanding where he was going with this.

He turned the stove off and faced me, abandoning

his bacon. His eyes were intent on mine, his mouth drawn and serious.

"You're not being yourself with her. You're holding back."

My brows rose. "And how would you know anything about that? Is this about what you said to her last night? I know you scared her again. She was practically shaking when she came downstairs for dinner. You have to stop fucking doing that. Ashlyn isn't from our world. She's innocent and gentle, and—"

"She's definitely innocent," he cut me off. "That's why you're so obsessed with her. You want her innocence."

"That's part of it," I admitted. "I like that she's not part of our world."

"That's not what I mean. You want to take that innocence. You want to corrupt her."

My fists curled at my sides. "I don't."

"Don't lie, Joseph. I know you better than anyone. You like that she's so sweet and pure, but you want her to be your dirty little angel, just for you."

"Fuck off." I couldn't hear more. I couldn't bear to hear the awful truth I'd been trying to deny. I wanted to shelter Ashlyn from all the ugly things in my life. I wasn't ashamed of my kinks, but I knew she would be frightened by them. I wouldn't do that to her.

"She saw my sketches," he announced, keeping me fixed in his implacable stare.

Anger surged. "You showed those to her?" Marco's sketches were supposed to be private, something only the two of us knew about.

"No. I found her snooping. She was staring at them, Joseph. She didn't know I was watching her. Those pretty pink lips were parted, her eyes wide. I could practically see her pulse jumping at her throat."

"Because she was scared. You scared her." If Marco was trying to allay my anger, he was only riling it.

"Maybe she was scared. Just a little. Just the right amount. You should have seen her, Joseph. She couldn't stop staring. And when I showed her the one of the two of you together, she licked her lips and blushed the prettiest shade of pink. I don't think she even realized it. She wants it, Joseph."

"She doesn't," I countered, even though something tugged in my chest. "She ran down here after. She was holding me so tight, and she was trembling."

"I like seeing a woman tremble," he said, his eyes sparking with a rare hint of light. I wasn't the only one who found Ashlyn's innocence alluring.

"She doesn't like you," I informed him, the words paining me. I hated that she seemed to dislike my best friend so much that she'd seek shelter from him in my arms. "You can't keep scaring her like this."

"She wasn't scared. Not of the drawings and not of me. She was scared of how they made her feel. Stop pretending to be someone you're not, Joseph. If you really are meant to be together, she'll accept you as you are. She'll welcome it."

"You don't know her like I do. You didn't know her in Cambridge. She's led a charmed life, Marco. I was relieved she wasn't a virgin. I thought she might be when I first met her. That's how innocent she is."

"And that's part of why you want her," he circled back around to the crux of his argument. "How long do you think you can keep fucking her like this?"

"Like what?"

"Like you're some vanilla, boring man with a vanilla, boring life. You might not like our violent world, but you do like your toys. You like playing with women, dominating them. You like the control. You know this about yourself. I know this about you. Ashlyn isn't made of glass. In fact, I'm sure she's quite flexible. Can't you imagine what she'd look like, tied up in your ropes?" His voice got rougher as he spoke, his dark words affecting him as much as they were tempting me.

"We can't," I forced out. "*I* can't. Ashlyn's not built for that kind of play."

"I think she is. I think she was made for it. She wouldn't be so infatuated with you, otherwise. I've seen the way she looks at you, the way she reacts when you touch her. Think about it, Joseph. She's innocent, but you could be the first one to corrupt her."

The first one? Fuck that. There wouldn't be anyone else in her future. She was staying here, with Marco and me.

"I don't want to discuss this anymore," I said in clipped tones. "I'm not going to do anything that might frighten her. She's scared enough as it is. A couple days ago, she was a normal college student whose biggest worry was studying for finals. Now, she's faced with the fact that she's caught in the middle of a war within our family. She's dealing with enough as it is. It's a miracle she's not trying to claw my eyes out for keeping her captive. She's agreed to stay here, under our protection. If that means I have to protect her from myself, from *us*, then that's what I'll do."

"You're making a mistake."

"Then it's my mistake to make. Ashlyn is my responsibility, Marco. Mine."

He flinched ever so slightly. If I hadn't known him so well, I wouldn't have noticed it.

I knew he was interested in her. Any man would

want her, but Ashlyn's innocence would call to him as strongly as it allured me. Marco's reasons for finding her appealing might be different from mine, but we'd always wanted the same women. That had never been a problem before. We liked to share.

But he didn't understand Ashlyn like I did. He didn't know her at all.

I'd do whatever it took to keep her happy, including denying my perversions and shielding her from Marco's darker urges.

Chapter Twenty-One
ASHLYN

A week had passed since I'd seen Marco's perverted drawings, but I still hadn't told Joseph about them. It would be weird to tell him about his friend's intimate, kinky sketches.

Wouldn't it?

I couldn't shake the image from my mind: Joseph looming behind me with a coil of rope. Every time he pinned me to the mattress or pushed me up against the wall, trapping me in place while he fucked me, the lewd drawing would pop into my head.

It was distracting.

Inappropriate.

And it always entered my mind right as I reached orgasm.

But I couldn't tell Joseph about it. He'd think I

was a pervert for even looking at Marco's drawings. I couldn't imagine what he'd say if I told him I thought about them when I climaxed.

Not to mention what it might do to their friendship if Joseph found out that Marco had drawn me like that, bound and naked. Joseph might not seem particularly possessive of me when his friend was around, but this was on a whole other level. I highly doubted Marco showed Joseph his sketches. It would be like sharing porn, and that was just weird. Men didn't do that.

Did they?

I supposed I didn't really know that much about men. I'd had one boyfriend for a month in junior year of high school, and I'd dated a guy freshman year of college—Jimmy. He'd cheated on me, so I'd ended the relationship. I hadn't really felt much of a connection, but the betrayal still stung. It only set me further back with my deeply ingrained trust issues.

I'd thought I could move past those issues when I'd first met Joseph, but it turned out he'd been deceiving me all along; he hadn't told me about his criminal lifestyle. There was honesty between us now, but I was still holding back my feelings for him. He hadn't fully earned my trust.

That barrier between us prevented me from

bringing up Marco's drawing. I couldn't reveal the depth of my depraved thoughts to Joseph. Not when I couldn't put my heart in his hands without hesitation or fear of getting hurt.

"What's wrong, angel?" Joseph called me out of my brooding thoughts.

"Nothing." I sighed and leaned my cheek against his shoulder, trying to focus on the TV again. We'd moved on from *Stranger Things* to *Sons of Anarchy*. I liked the show, but it wasn't enough to hold my attention when I couldn't get that lewd drawing out of my head.

Joseph picked up the remote and turned off the TV. He took my hands in his, staring into my eyes as though he could read my thoughts if he just looked hard enough.

"You're not happy," he finally said. "What can I do?"

I shifted, uncomfortable with his scrutiny. I cut my eyes away, unable to bear the weight of his crystalline stare.

"It's just... I don't know," I hedged. "It's hard being away from school." That much was true. I was stressing about falling behind on my coursework, and while I loved being with Joseph, I was feeling a little cooped up in the big, empty mansion.

"Do you think Marco has scheduled for the pool to be filled yet?" I asked, hopeful. If I could just go for a nice, long swim, I could clear my mind.

"I'm not sure. I'll ask him again."

This would be the third time Joseph had to ask about it. I wasn't sure why Marco was dragging his feet. It shouldn't be hard for someone with his kind of money to get the pool cleaned and filled in a few days.

"Thanks," I said, holding in my irritation. It wasn't Joseph's fault that Marco wasn't as concerned with my happiness as he was. Joseph adored me, pampered me. There was no reason for me to expect the same kind of treatment from Marco. He'd barely looked at me since I'd seen his sketches. I would've thought he was embarrassed, but he didn't strike me as the type to get embarrassed. He certainly hadn't seemed at all ashamed when he'd commanded me to turn the page and look at his drawing of Joseph tying me up.

The memory made my face heat.

Joseph's gaze flicked to my pink cheeks and back to my eyes. A furrow appeared between his brows as he studied me, as though I was a puzzle he couldn't quite figure out.

"I'm going to take you out to dinner," he

announced. "You must be getting tired of being on the estate. I know Marco is a great cook, but I think you need to get out for a little while."

"Yes," I agreed quickly. I really did want to get out of this house. It was huge and lonely, but on the rare occasions when Marco was in the room with us, it somehow seemed stiflingly small.

Joseph beamed at me, and I found myself grinning back. He was beautiful when he smiled, his sensual features lighting up with joy. I could hardly believe that this gorgeous, kind man was mine.

I closed the distance between us, initiating our kiss. His lips were still curved with pleasure when they met mine. I melted against him, losing myself in his arms for the rest of the afternoon.

∽

"Why is he here?" I whispered in Joseph's ear once Marco got out of the car. He'd driven us here in his shiny black BMW, and Joseph and I sat in the backseat. I caught his hand, lingering in the privacy of the car for a few seconds.

"He's here to protect you, just like I am." Joseph squeezed my hand. "And this will be good. We can all have dinner together, and you'll get to know him better. He's not as scary as you think he is. At least, not where you're concerned."

Before I could say that I'd wanted to have a romantic date alone with Joseph, Marco opened the car door for me.

He held out a hand to help me out of the car. Since Joseph was getting out on the other side, I didn't have the option of clinging to him. It would be rude not to take Marco's gentlemanly assistance.

Even if I didn't want it. I didn't like being near him. It was...uncomfortable. Overwhelming.

I sucked in a breath when his thick fingers closed around my hand, engulfing my palm. It was the first time he'd touched me since the night he'd abducted me —when he'd trapped me against the wall and pressed his hand over my mouth to smother my screams.

A shiver raced through me at the memory, but he wasn't acting aggressive right now. He held my hand as carefully as Joseph always did, as though he might accidentally break my fingers if he squeezed too hard.

He probably could.

I got to my feet, and Marco closed the car door behind me. He didn't release my hand.

I glanced up at him, and I found his black eyes burning down into me. His nostrils flared, like a predator scenting his prey.

I didn't try to pull away. I couldn't. All I could do was stand there, trapped in his dark stare. I felt small and helpless in his shadow, his huge hand on mine a reminder of his massive size in comparison to my much smaller body.

Joseph's hand touched my lower back, and heat flooded my body at the familiar, intimate contact. The electric attraction that always danced around us surged, making the fine hairs on the back of my neck stand on end. My hand tingled in Marco's, and I became very aware of the heat of their bodies surrounding me, shielding me from the chilly night air.

Despite the warmth, I shivered. The corners of Marco's mouth curved, and streetlights caught in his dark eyes, flashing across his onyx stare. His thumb brushed my knuckles, and I drew in a sharp, shocked breath at the light caress.

Joseph was standing right beside me, but he must not have noticed. He couldn't have, or he would say something. He wouldn't allow Marco to touch me like that.

He's just holding my hand, a more rational voice in my mind reminded me. There was no reason for Joseph to get territorial over something so trivial.

I tugged my hand free from Marco's grip, as

though he'd scalded me. His expression went carefully blank, and he stepped away. Joseph's touch on my lower back firmed, steering me toward the restaurant.

It was a small, quaint Italian place set on the main street of a little town near Marco's estate. I still wasn't sure exactly where it was located, but it had only taken us ten minutes to drive here. We weren't as isolated as I'd thought we might be. I hadn't seen a soul except Joseph and Marco since they'd taken me from school, and I'd assumed we were in the middle of nowhere.

Marco's family must be even wealthier than I'd imagined if they owned that much land so close to a heavily populated area. The real estate must be worth a fortune.

When we entered the restaurant, a pretty brunette showed us to our table—for three.

It was strange being seated in an intimate corner with both Joseph and Marco. I glanced around, wondering what people must think of us. Surely, the other patrons thought it was odd, too.

But no one in the packed restaurant seemed to be sparing us a second glance.

Well, that wasn't exactly accurate. A balding, middle-aged man caught my eye as I looked around.

After a second of eye contact, his genial expression melted, and he paled. He quickly looked away.

I glanced up to find Marco scowling at the man. His face was harder than I'd ever seen it, the harsh line of his square jaw set and his cold eyes narrowed.

He must have felt my gaze on him, because he blinked once and looked back at me. The fierce expression was gone in an instant. He didn't smile at me, but he wasn't scowling, either. I realized that the neutral expression he usually wore must be his default. I'd thought he was trying to be intimidating when his face was carefully blank. But I'd just seen his actual intimidating expression, and the neutral one was practically a silly grin in comparison.

I fiddled with the napkin in my lap to hide my trembling fingers beneath the table. Marco was even scarier than I'd imagined.

The server came by to take our order. Before I could look at the menu, Marco barked out a list of dishes that could probably feed five people.

"That's a lot of food," I remarked when the server left.

He shrugged. "I'm hungry. And this way, you can try some of everything."

"Oh." He still wasn't smiling, but that seemed like a nice thing to say. Like he cared about whether or not I enjoyed my dinner. "Okay. Thanks."

He tipped his head in a slight nod, acknowledging my response.

Joseph's fingers laced with mine beneath the table, stopping me from picking at my napkin. My anxiety mostly melted away at his reassuring touch.

"Ashlyn was asking about the pool earlier," Joseph told Marco. "Any progress on that?"

Marco's granite jaw firmed, and his eyes narrowed on Joseph. I would have scooted away if he'd turned that glare on me, but Joseph didn't seem affected. I supposed he was used to it.

"Well, keep me updated," Joseph said when Marco didn't deign to answer. "It's really important to Ashlyn."

Marco's eyes riveted on me again, and I shifted in my seat. He wasn't glaring anymore, but his gaze was...intense. I wanted to look away, but that strange sensation of being trapped by his stare alone kept me locked in place.

"Why *Number1unicorn!*?" he asked.

I blinked. "What?" I said, a bit breathlessly. It was the last thing I'd expected him to say. I'd thought we were about to have an argument about the pool.

"Your password," he prompted. "Why did you choose *Number1unicorn!*? I'm assuming the university didn't assign it to you."

"Oh. Well." I shifted nervously. Joseph's fingers

firmed on mine, grounding me. "I guess I just, um, I like unicorns?" The last came out as a question.

The corners of Marco's mouth curved again. "What do you like about them?"

"What?" I was acting like a total idiot who couldn't carry a conversation, but this entire line of questioning was baffling. Why would Marco care about my interest in unicorns, of all things?

"You heard me." His voice came out in a rich, deep tone I'd never heard from him before. It was much warmer than anything he'd ever said, but somehow more...powerful.

"Well, they're beautiful." The words tumbled out of my mouth. "And, I don't know, magical. I just like the idea of them. I guess it's a nostalgia thing."

A single dark brow rose, prompting me to elaborate. "A nostalgia thing?"

That commanding tone did something to my insides. Tendrils of warmth unfurled in my chest, and my explanation of my silly password became an effusive confession of my lifelong obsession with all things whimsical and beautiful. "I used to love the movie *The Last Unicorn* growing up. I'd watch it all the time. I had every unicorn-themed Lisa Frank folder when I was in elementary school. And I was obsessed with *Rainbow Brite* because of Starlite. But Starlite isn't actually a unicorn. He's still magical, though."

I pressed my lips together, smothering my ridiculous babbling. It wasn't uncommon for me to talk enthusiastically about the things I loved if I was around people I trusted. But even Jayme didn't know the extent of my unicorn craze.

Marco's onyx eyes flicked from my pursed lips to my flame-red cheeks, and a bright grin suddenly illuminated his rough-hewn features.

I blinked, dumbstruck.

Marco was grinning. Actually grinning. And it wasn't the scary, sharply amused smile I'd seen him wear before. This was a genuine smile, and it reached his eyes. They crinkled at the corners, and dark-chocolate warmth melted the hard, cold light that usually reflected off them.

I'd never appreciated how ruggedly handsome Marco was. I'd been fully aware of his masculine physique, and I'd picked each of his harsh features apart in moments of fear. But when he smiled like this, he didn't seem all that frightening. He was magnetic, compelling.

"I need the bathroom," I said suddenly, almost surprising myself. Sitting so close to Marco was too... Well, I didn't exactly feel uncomfortable around him right now. It was more...intense. Sitting close to Marco was intense.

"We'll be right here, angel," Joseph said, squeezing my hand one last time before releasing it.

I popped up out of my chair and hurried to the bathroom. Embarrassingly, I ended up getting a little lost looking for it. The brunette who'd showed us to our table directed me from the front of the restaurant back toward the kitchen. The ladies' room was down a long hall to the left. Luckily, it was far out of sight from Joseph and Marco, so they hadn't seen me wandering around like an idiot. I'd already made enough of a fool of myself, talking to Marco about unicorns.

And what the hell had all that been about? Why would Marco care about me liking unicorns? It was a silly, childish thing, and I was a little embarrassed by it. There was a reason I'd chosen it for my password: passwords are secret.

Even though I hadn't particularly needed to go, I used the facilities and washed my hands. When I'd dried them, I lingered in front of the mirror for a minute longer, willing the pink blush to subside from my cheeks. My body was hot, flushed. It was cold outside, but I'd been far too overheated when surrounded by Joseph's and Marco's bulk.

Ice water, I told myself. *I need ice water.*

I unlocked the bathroom door and took a few more seconds to smooth my hair back from my face.

I heaved in a deep breath, bracing myself to return to the table.

I wasn't sure why I felt the need to brace myself. Joseph was there, waiting for me. He would make sure I was safe and happy.

The bathroom door swung open, and I jolted.

"Occupied," I said, but the lady didn't seem to care.

No. It wasn't a lady.

A man stepped into the small, tiled space. He was almost as tall as Joseph, even if he wasn't as broad. He looked leaner. Scrappier. Meaner.

His lips were curled in a sneer, and a wicked scar on his right cheek puckered from his twisted expression.

"This is the ladies' room," I said, trying not to stare at his scar.

He shut the door behind him. Locked it.

"I wanted to talk to you, Ashlyn." He took a step toward me.

I jolted back, and my butt hit the wall. The space was too small, and the man was too close.

Before I could open my mouth to scream for Joseph, the man pulled aside his leather jacket to reveal a gun holstered at his side. He pressed his finger against his lips as he shushed me.

"What do you want?" I whispered, not daring to

raise my voice any louder. "How do you know my name?"

"I know a lot of things about you." He took another step toward me, but there was nowhere for me to go, nowhere to run. "Not as much as Joseph knows about you, judging by the pictures my friends took." He reached up and brushed his knuckles down my cheek.

I turned my face away, but he didn't break contact. My heart hammered against my ribs, fear coursing through my veins. It was just as toxic as it had been the night Marco kidnapped me. Only, this man wasn't reassuring me that he would take me to Joseph and keep me safe.

He traced the line of my jaw before picking up a lock of my hair. He lifted it to his nose and inhaled deeply. I shuddered, feeling more violated than I had when he'd touched my face.

"You're very pretty," he told me. "I can see why Joseph likes you. I'm sure he'd be heartbroken if anything happened to you."

A soft knock sounded against the door. "Ashlyn?"

"Joseph!" I gasped out his name, too breathless to scream for him.

A loud *bang* echoed through the bathroom as the door flew open, the wood splintering around the broken lock. Joseph slammed into the man who'd been threatening me, his momentum taking them both to the floor.

I shrieked when strong arms grabbed me.

"It's me," Marco said. "I've got you."

He picked me up, cradling me against his chest as he turned me away from the violence. Joseph brought his fist down on the man's nose. I saw blood spray, and I hid my face against Marco's neck.

"Don't kill him, Joseph," Marco warned as he carried me away. "We can't draw first blood."

Marco rushed through the restaurant. His big body shielded mine as he held me close, his huge arms protecting me. Several patrons exclaimed and a few stood to gawk, but Marco didn't seem to care. He was completely focused on getting me away from the man who'd scared me.

"Wait!" I twisted in his arms when cool night air kissed my skin. "Joseph." We couldn't leave him behind. "That man had a gun." My panic spiked, and I squirmed against Marco's hold.

"He won't use it," Marco promised me. "They were just trying to send a message. Joseph will be fine."

"You can't know that!" I continued struggling, but his arms were iron around me.

"He's already behind us."

I listened, registering heavy footfalls racing

toward us. I craned my head back to look over Marco's shoulder.

"Joseph!" I practically sobbed his name as relief ripped through me.

"I'll drive," Joseph told Marco as he caught up to us. "You cover her."

Marco nodded, shifting me slightly so he could open the back door of the BMW. He slid inside with me, placing me on my back along the seat. I heard Joseph slam the driver's side door, and the car lurched forward. Marco leaned over me, his weight pressing me down into the leather as his body covered mine.

"That's it," he said, his voice low and soothing. "Hold on to me. You're safe."

I didn't realize my fingers had curled into the front of his shirt, and I was holding on to him for dear life.

Marco's huge hands started roving over my body with shocking gentleness. "Did he touch you? Did he hurt you?" Despite his gentle hands, his words were a rough growl.

"N-no," I stammered, my teeth clicking together. It was so cold in the car. "He just said..." I trailed off, shivering at the memory of the man's hand on my face.

"What did he say?" Marco prompted.

"He knew my name. He said his friends had

pictures of Joseph and me together. He said Joseph would be upset if anything happened to me."

Joseph's harsh curse floated back to me, and the engine roared as the car picked up speed.

"We're through the gates," he announced a few minutes later. He must have smashed the speed limit to get us back to the estate so quickly.

Marco finally sat up, pulling me with him so I sat in his lap. He held me close and placed his hand on the side of my head, tucking my face against his chest. My fingers were still fisted in his shirt, but he didn't seem to mind. He rubbed my chilled arms with his free hand, and he stroked my hair with the other.

"It's okay, princess. I know that was scary, but you're safe now."

I nodded against him, soothed by the deep timbre of his voice. I was so rattled by what had happened, I didn't even register the strange fact that I was feeling comforted by Marco. Just a few hours ago, I'd found him frightening.

But there was nothing scary about the way he held me, warming my chilled skin with his body heat. Tears spilled from my eyes, wetting his shirt.

"You can cry," he assured me. "Hold on to me and cry. You'll feel better after."

I let the tears flow freely as I purged the residual

fear from my system. I was safe in his strong arms, and I didn't have to be afraid of him anymore.

Joseph had been right all along. Marco only wanted to keep me safe. They'd both warned me that if I tried to leave the estate, their enemies would find me. Until now, I hadn't really understood the threat. I'd believed that Joseph was somehow involved with the mafia, and I'd heard him loud and clear when he'd told me that he had enemies.

Do you want to be murdered? Or maybe they'll just rape you. Or maybe they'll pass you around until they get bored, and then they'll kill you. Marco's blunt description of what their enemies might do to me thundered through my mind, sending shockwaves of panic shuddering through my body.

You're very pretty. I can see why Joseph likes you. I'm sure he'd be heartbroken if anything happened to you. The scarred man's words layered over my memory of Marco's warning, and my cheek burned where their enemy had brushed his knuckles over my skin.

I buried my face against Marco's chest, as though his steady heat could melt away the taint of my attacker's touch. Suddenly, this world of mobsters and mortal danger was very real. The gates that guarded Marco's estate felt less like the bars of a cage and more like a defensive barricade.

Any fantasies I'd entertained about quickly

returning to Harvard evaporated. From now on, I had to trust Joseph and Marco to keep me safe.

We would remain on this estate indefinitely. Together. The three of us.

∼

Thank you for reading MAFIA CAPTIVE!
Joseph, Ashlyn, and Marco's story continues in
THE DADDY AND THE DOM.

THE DADDY AND THE DOM EXCERPT

Ashlyn

My frozen skin was icier than the cold tiles at my back, a searing contrast to the heated blood that pounded a head-splitting drumbeat in my ears. My racing heart slammed against my ribcage, inflicting a bruising ache deep in my chest.

The wicked scar carved into my attacker's face twisted on a leer, and his hot breath burned my frozen cheeks. His wiry body pressed into mine, the sharp edges of his joints pinning me in place. Something hard jammed into my side: the gun he'd used to threaten me and compel my silence.

All my muscles locked up with the sudden, primal knowledge of mortal danger. One wrong move, and a bullet would tear through my stomach.

He leaned in close, his rough stubble scraping my cheek.

"You're very pretty." His oily words oozed over my neck, leaving a toxic trail. "I can see why Joseph likes you. I'm sure he'd be heartbroken if anything happened to you."

Sticky warmth painted my skin, and when he pulled away, his face was a gory mess. Blood spilled over his thin lips, cut raw by his broken, jagged teeth.

Joseph had done that. He'd smashed the man's jaw when he'd come to my defense.

Horror was a lead weight in my stomach, and I managed to tear my eyes from the nauseating sight of his ruined face. Frantically, I searched the cramped bathroom for my savior, the man I loved.

But Joseph wasn't there. I was alone with this monstrous man, completely powerless to escape him.

"You're very pretty," he said again, his tone roughed with sick hunger. "Maybe I'll pass you around to my friends until they get bored, and then I'll kill you."

Shadows thickened in the corners of the small space, growing into dark, indistinct silhouettes of towering men.

A second hard length pressed into my hip, larger than the gun shoved into my side.

I thrashed like a trapped animal, and my shriek

echoed through the bathroom, rebounding against the tiles to pierce my eardrums. The shadows closed in on me, trailing frozen fingers over my flesh.

My wordless scream coalesced into Joseph's name, begging for him to save me...

"Ashlyn! Wake up, angel." The strong fingers that closed around my shoulders were warm and calloused; nothing like the icy, grasping claws of my shadowy attackers.

My eyes snapped open, and I finally found the intense, flame-blue stare of my savior.

"Joseph!" I half-sobbed his name and buried my face against his chest, breathing in his comforting, masculine scent.

His steady heat sank into my frigid flesh, but the shadows still clung to my mind with icy, dark tendrils. I pressed closer to him, struggling to fully surface from the nightmare and ground myself in the safety of his strong arms.

I barely had time to register two of Joseph's thundering heartbeats beneath my ear before a deafening *bang* tore through the room. The feel of my attacker's gun was a phantom pain rammed into my side. The terror that'd barely begun to ebb away surged again, and I cried out as the nightmare eclipsed reality.

"Jesus, Marco!" Joseph snapped. He pulled me tighter to his chest, and the pressure of his muscular arms around my shaking body reassured me of his protective presence. "It's okay, angel," he murmured, pressing a tender kiss to my forehead. "You're safe."

"I heard screaming." The rough growl should've made my insides quake, but I recognized Marco's rumbling voice.

My face lifted from Joseph's chest, my eyes searching for my other fierce savior. I hadn't longed for Marco in my dream, but now that his powerful aura pulsed into the room, I was desperate to catch sight of him. I wanted to reassure myself that he was real, too. That both of these immensely strong men were here to shelter me, like they'd promised.

My eyes found Marco, and my breath caught in my throat. His ripped, muscular body was impossibly broader and more intimidating than I'd ever realized. His sculpted chest was bare, and his defined abs bunched tight with coiled aggression. He wore nothing but a pair of black sweatpants slung low on his hips. His massive physique was on full, hulking display.

The sight of his towering frame swelling to fill the doorway should've been scary as hell, but I released a shuddering sigh as relief rolled through me.

"It was just a nightmare." Joseph addressed Marco in clipped tones, and he pulled me closer to his hard body.

The cold light that glittered over Marco's obsidian eyes melted, and the ferocious snarl eased from his rough-hewn features. "You had a nightmare, princess?"

He took a step toward me, and my surroundings finally solidified. I was in Marco's bedroom, where I'd been sleeping with Joseph.

At some point after he'd whisked me away from the dangerous encounter at the restaurant, Marco had carried me up here and tucked me beneath the plush duvet, ensuring I was warm after my bone-chilling confrontation with their enemy. I barely remembered falling asleep in Joseph's arms, exhausted and shaky from the frightening experience.

The trauma of being cornered and threatened by a mobster must've followed me down into sleep, triggering my night terror.

Marco took another step toward me, moving with slow, easy grace that was entirely at odds with the pure menace that'd rolled off him in waves only seconds ago. He'd stormed in here and rushed to my defense after hearing me scream.

I noticed the dent in the wall behind him, where he'd flung open the door with enough force that the brass handle had damaged the plaster. All that strength, all that ferocity...

For me. He'd come running to protect me the moment he'd thought I was in danger.

My stomach did a funny flip, and a small shiver raced over my skin. I wasn't scared of Marco. Not at all. But this display of his brute strength and intense protectiveness made me quake for darker, more feminine reasons.

Joseph misinterpreted my trembling and rubbed his big hands over my pebbled flesh. My cheeks burned as I realized I was ogling Marco while clinging to Joseph. I tucked my face closer to his chest, hiding my confusing response to his best friend's powerful presence.

"I've got this, Marco." Joseph's warning words rumbled through the room.

Marco's low grunt snagged my attention, and my eyes were immediately drawn to him once again. He'd stopped dead in his tracks, still as a granite statue. His jaw ticked, and his black eyes raked over my trembling body before returning to my face. He studied me with that unwavering, penetrating stare for several unnerving seconds.

His fists flexed at his sides just once before he gave Joseph a curt nod and turned on his heel.

"Wait!" I called out, the plea bursting from my aching chest before I could think better of it. Less than a minute ago, Marco had been all softness and concern when he'd asked about my nightmare. Now, he was stiff and cold again. Aloof after Joseph's sharp dismissal.

Joseph thought he was sheltering me from further distress, but Marco was the one who was upset.

Something tugged at my heart when his hulking body jerked to a halt, and he turned back to face me. His dark brows were drawn low over his eyes, the glower shielding him from me.

But that glower didn't frighten me anymore. I'd seen him turn the same ferocious expression on Joseph when he was upset, not enraged.

"Thank you," I said softly, compelled to convey my gratitude and my newfound trust in him. My belief that he wasn't an evil criminal.

I'd been so blind to his better nature, simmering in resentment over his decision to kidnap me. But when he'd comforted me in the car last night, letting me cry against him as he held me with aching gentleness, I'd finally understood why Joseph cared so much about his intimidating friend.

Fine lines appeared around Marco's mouth on a small frown, and he cocked his head at me.

"Thank you for coming to check on me," I explained. "And for getting me away from...that man." I shuddered at the memory of their enemy's knuckles raking down my cheek in a perversion of intimacy.

Joseph's long, sure fingers trailed through my hair in comforting strokes, and I relaxed into his arms as the last of my residual terror drained from my system. Suddenly, exhaustion sank into my bones, and my head felt too heavy to stir.

The warmth returned to Marco's eyes, and he relaxed, too. "Go back to sleep, princess. I'm right down the hall if you need me. I won't let anyone hurt you."

"I know," I murmured, my eyelids growing heavier with each stroke of Joseph's fingers through my hair. "Thank you."

His answering, low hum followed me down into warm darkness, and I slept peacefully through the night.

Joseph, Ashlyn, and Marco's story continues in **THE DADDY AND THE DOM**

ALSO BY JULIA SYKES

Mafia Ménage Trilogy

Mafia Captive

The Daddy and The Dom

Theirs to Protect

The Captive Series

Sweet Captivity

Claiming My Sweet Captive

Stealing Beauty

Captive Ever After

Pretty Hostage

Wicked King

Ruthless Savior

The Impossible Series

Impossible

Savior

Rogue

Knight

Mentor

Master

King

A Decadent Christmas (An Impossible Series Christmas Special)

Czar

Crusader

Prey (An Impossible Series Short Story)

Highlander

Decadent Knights (An Impossible Series Short Story)

Centurion

Dex

Hero

Wedding Knight (An Impossible Series Short Story)

Valentines at Dusk (An Impossible Series Short Story)

Nice & Naughty (An Impossible Series Christmas Special)

Dark Lessons

RENEGADE

The Dark Grove Plantation Series

Holden

Brandon

Damien

Printed in Great Britain
by Amazon